Slaves & Breeders

by

J.D. GRAYSON

49,000 words

2015 Gray Publishing Paperback Edition

Copyright © 2013 by J.D. Grayson

ISBN 978-1939496324

CONTENTS

All books are now available in Paperback. For autographed copies
please send your request to JDGrayson@hotmail.com

Visit J.D. Grayson's website to signup for a new release alerts.

Website: www.JDGraysonBooks.com

Twitter: @JDGraysonBooks

Part One

Abducted into Sex Slavery

CHAPTER ONE

Craigslist Ad:
Do you want to be a supermodel? If so, just respond to this ad! I'm
currently seeking curvy models to shoot for a major modeling firm. I
will personally photograph you, immediately send the specs to my
agency, and your fate will be decided in minutes. Sound good? I
await your emails, girls.

*****

"I'm gonna be a supermodel!" Haley White assured herself. The redheaded, 21 year-old gazed into a full-length mirror. Her heart beat rapidly. A pair of teal eyes scanned her naked skin for blemishes. Even moles would be concealed.

Basically, she searched for signs of humanity. Of course, she was clueless that her idolized cover girls were airbrushed fakes. In reality, she didn't have to search, already knowing where her *problem areas* were. Identifying imperfection was a hobby of hers.

Haley's one hope lied in the encouragement of past boyfriends, declaring her model-like beauty.

Her fire-red nails matched the blazing tone of her hair. A trim sprinkling of ginger pubes remained. She connected the faint freckles upon her pale skin, wishing they were absent. Smoother than vanilla custard, her fingertips examined each killer curve.

Outlining her natural D-cup breasts, childbearing-hips, and pear-shaped bottom, Haley White fit the ad's criteria like a snug condom. Naive in nature, she failed to question the absence of a picture request.

Since high self-esteem was more rare than curvy modeling gigs, her sudden optimism overlooked such details. Being only 5'6, most ads called for tall, anorexic skeletons with boyish chests. The opposite of herself.

As each hour ticked by, new doubt emerged. *What if I'm not good enough? What if they think I'm ugly...reject me on the spot? I'll be so embarrassed, totally ruined. Stop it!* She chastised herself. *Models have confidence, attitude, swagger. I'm used to faking strength...this should come natural!*

Taking a last look into the mirror, she took a deep breath. There was more riding on *that* moment than just a modeling gig. It was more than stardom. The prize she sought was self-worth.

Having grown up in a vicious foster-care system, she trickled through the cracks. When she wasn't being teased by fellow orphans, she was ignored by social workers. After bouncing around a series of foster homes, the troubled teen finally found one to keep her.

However, unlike the punishments of the past, *that* home featured discipline by spanking. Her foster-father did it often, over the clothes. In her mind, a dark part of her wished for bare skin blows. The humiliating act turned her on, only causing her to act out more.

The day she turned 18, Haley decided to conquer two fantasies at once. Her foster-father was reading in his study, as the towel-wrapped teen approached him. "I'm finally outta here today!" she shouted.

"That's your right. You're an adult now...of age, not mentality," he said in mockery.

"I'm old enough to know...you can't spank me anymore, asshole."

He slowly lifted his head, shooting her a stern look. "While you're under my roof, I *can* do what I wish," he challenged. "Eighteen or not!"

The opportunistic girl dropped her towel, revealing her hourglass body. "I dare you to try," she threatened.

Speechless, the man's lustful eyes spoke for him. It wasn't the first time he saw the sight. Whether sneaking a peek at her changing, or creeping through her panty drawer while she slept, it was a long time coming.

In an animalistic rage, he lunged for her. Gripping his foster daughter by the arms, he forced her over his knee. The first slap was harder than ever. Apparently, bare butt spankings hurt more than clothed ones.

Haley squealed, caught between pleasure and pain. The tough girl suddenly felt fear, no longer protected under an umbrella of youth. She was now accountable for her actions.

Her foster father lifted his hand, letting forth another aggressive smack. His finger penetrated her cheeks, stinging her vaginal lips. The entrance to her secret lair jiggled, rimmed with white. Large red handprints covered her pale canvas, tingling more each time. The harder he hit, the harder she pressed into his erect cock. It appeared he was living out his own fantasy as well.

The punishment continued for another ten minutes. Hung over his lap, her dangling breasts reached for the floor. With every spank, her nipples were further inverted into the wood surface.

Haley finally broke. She cried out, grinding against his steel manhood, writhing in horrific embarrassment. Chills crawled through her body. Cumming so hard she left a small puddle upon his lap. The punishment continued, making her spasms uncontainable.

She halted her first real orgasm. After finishing, she remained quiet, unwilling to move. Haley finally broke in another way, crying her eyes out. For the first time, her weakness was exposed. Suddenly, the punisher gripped her, emulating her grinding movement. Panic filled her, realizing he was now cumming.

Soft, wet spurts seeped through his pants, staining Haley's thighs with strained semen. Feeling his cock twitch against her womanly womb, she paused in confusion. *Why did I get off on being spanked? Why did he get off on spanking me?*

Haley pondered. Although she didn't quite understand it, she discovered the force that triggered their pleasure. She orgasmed from being controlled, while he got off on the power his control unleashed. Although different, they were born of the same root. It was her first introduction to a dominant-submissive relationship.

Quickly rising, she grabbed her towel, wiping the joint lust from her thighs. Running to her room, she threw on clothes, grabbing pre-packed things. At that moment, Haley White entered the real world. She realized the tough girl was just a shell encasing the weak one. The moment frightened her to the core.

Forced to take small jobs for small money, her life was directionless and lonely. A few failed relationships fizzled out. Ready to better herself, the trouble girl was prepared to take initiative. However, opportunity wasn't awaiting her. With nothing to lose, the Craigslist ad paved the way forward.

Ending her mirror inspection, Haley squeezed a body-fitting dress on. Not wasting time with a bra or panties, she wanted the snug stocking to hug every asset. Her juicy nipples protruded, advertising teardrop-shaped breasts. With only one shot at the gig, she wasn't going to misfire.

"This is your chance," she told the girl in the mirror. "Win for once." Securing a pair of sexy, sharp heels, Ms. White grabbed her purse. Turning off the light, she approached fate.

*****

Stepping off the city bus, she exited into uncomfortable surroundings. The object of feminine desire had no car or friends to drop her off. She limped her way through busy streets, which were slowly coming alive.

"How much?" a thug taunted her.

"Excuse me?" she asked.

"How much for a blow job?"

"I'm not a prostitute!" she shouted, hurrying away from him. His laughter echoed through her ears.

The nervous girl continued to search the addresses. Arriving at a random warehouse, she squinted in wonderment. *Could this really be it? I guess photo shoots do use spaces like this. There's no turning back,* she thought, entering through the door.

Arriving in a large open room, she looked at her cellphone clock. It was 11 P.M. on the dot. She was on schedule. "Hello?" she shouted, causing her voice to echo.

"You must be Haley," a deep, male voice startled her from behind.

The edgy redhead gasped, quickly turning around. A 40 year old, 6'3 man appeared. He had strong arms and a trusting face. His dark, slicked hair contrasted deep blue eyes. A squared, heroic chin framed cheek stubble. "You scared me. Yeah, I'm...Haley. Haley White."

The man was momentarily breathless. Having seen many girls, there was something about Haley that struck him. *That face,* he silently thought. *It's almost as if she's been resurrected...no!* He chastised himself. *Don't do this. It'll only make the job harder.* "Bruce Knight," he said, holding out his hand.

She took it, feeling his strong grip. Looking around, she asked, "I'm sorry for asking, but...where's the photo equipment?"

Bruce flashed a smile, walking over to a switch. After one flip, two bright spotlights were activated. A camera, tripod, and white-sheeted backdrop were revealed.

Haley exhaled, relaxing. "Just checking."

"Did you doubt me?"

"No, never. It's just the Internet...you never really know who you're talking to. Or what someone's motives are."

"I can't blame you for that. Is anyone with you today? Friend...family member?"

"Nope, I'm alone like you requested." *He doesn't need to know my loneliness isn't a choice,* she thought.

"Perfect. Did you keep this little meeting quiet?"

"Didn't tell a soul for this...*top secret project*. Just as you insisted."

"Very good," Bruce said. "Just to reconfirm your email...no husband...never had children?"

"Nope, single and childless. Are you sure I don't need prior experience? I don't even have a portfolio," she asked.

"Is this the way you sell yourself to everyone...or just me?"

"Pretty pathetic I guess, eh?"

"Give yourself more credit...I've only seen such natural beauty once before," he said, failing to explain. Haley smiled, blushing at the rare comment. Arriving at the photo set up, he said, "We'll get some hot shots...send them in…and the rest is up to them."

"Them?"

"The company."

"Do you mind if I ask...their name, location, basic info? Just to settle my curiosity?"

Now Bruce seemed off-guard. "Well...we like to keep that info quiet, until the model is chosen. I'll tell you this though...we're located on a beautiful island. One foot on its sands...you'll never leave."

Excitement filled Haley's naive face. "Really? Sounds cool. I've never traveled overseas. To be honest, I've never even left the state of Florida."

"Then let's get this new life started."

After she struck some random poses, the camera busily recorded Haley's moves. Though, Bruce's face soured upon viewing his digital creations.

"I'm not good enough?" a disappointed Haley asked.

"At this level...it's not a question of good. It's a question of great. You're up against a thousand other girls here."

"What will it take...I'll do anything?"

Bruce delivered the usual script. "I know what they look for. It's something no other girl's done today."

"Please, tell me."

"Remove your clothes."

Haley gasped. "But...I don't do nudes. I want a legitimate modeling career."

"And this is the way to get one," he said. "Don't believe what you read in the glamour mags...all the greats started this way."

She exhaled again. "I just wanted to change my ways..."

"Forget it. We'll just do it your way," he said, returning to his camera.

"Wait!" the desperate girl shouted. "I'll do it."

Bruce nodded, expecting to hear her response. He'd done it so many times in his life, any pleasure was gone. As much as he hated to admit it, the guilt remained. Letting the camera hang upon his neck, he gripped the frilled edges of Haley's red dress. "Lift your hands up into the air."

The nervous girl paused, exhaling. *This is for stardom. Let's just hope not porn-stardom,* she thought, remembering what her foster-father always said. 'You'll end up in one of those slut films!' She banished all thoughts from her mind. Following his command, her arms went upward.

Bruce's large, powerful hands lifted her dress. Brushing her inner thighs with his thumbs, a tickling sensation pinged her vaginal nerves. Continuing on, he arrived at the edge of her puffed lips. The stiff girl gasped, feeling him smear her wet folds together.

Tracing the lips, he teased a trail through her faint red fibers, unveiling womanly hips. Passing her belly button, he freed her D-Cup breasts, letting them breathe the stale air.

As he worked the dress over Haley's head, his body pressed against hers. The stranger's thick cock bumped her womanhood, begging to claim it. By the time her dress cleared the extended arms, Ms. White's curves were pushed outward, bulged to their limits.

Bruce tossed the dress far from her reach. It was as if she wouldn't need it again. The exposed young woman immediately covered her intimate areas. As the photographer stepped backward, he said, "Not gonna work."

Knowing she had to comply, Haley dropped her guard. Her feminine glory was revealed, awakening Bruce's deepest desires. "I'm not used to this," she said in embarrassment. "At least...not for multiple eyes."

"Don't worry, it's only for the eyes of one other. Head up." Haley's head rose, looking into the camera lens. Her glassy form reflected back. As awkward as she felt, the sight swept her like a lusty wave. "It's time to perform," Bruce demanded.

Abandoning all fear, Haley immediately placed her hands behind her head, accentuating her luscious breasts. The camera's digital snap devoured beauty, as the flash illuminated milky skin. "Is this good?" she asked.

"More," he encouraged her.

She formed other seductive positions, warming to the process. Noticing Bruce's erection, her confidence was only boosted further. The more the camera captured her, the more her inhibition vanished.

"So sexy!" He snapped the shutter furiously. Raising the stakes, he pulled a blanket off the backdrop, laying it down. "Sprawl," he ordered. The heated girl obeyed. Her guarded submissive nature was unleashed to its fullest, surpassing her foster-father's lap.

Ms. White stretched upon the white sheet, following Bruce's every order. "Spread your legs," he boldly ordered. Haley was about to descend from soft core to hard. However, she was so hot at that moment, only his command mattered. Her thighs opened, flashing her garden of gummy goodness.

"Touch yourself!" he instructed. Haley surrendered all thought, roving her luscious skin. Rubbing her breasts, she squeezed and massaged the mighty mounds. Sliding down her soft stomach, her red fingernails carved her curved hips, following the natural path to her creamy thighs. "Now...take the final step. Pleasure yourself!"

Swearing not to cross that line, her willpower crumbled. She'd come too far to turn back. Abandoning all principle, she dipped her fingers into the dripping lips. Pulling them wide apart, her tender red flesh was strung with human glue. Pinching her clitoris, she swirled two fingers like a feather-bladed blender.

Her opposite hand wiggled three fingers into her love canal, feeding the hungry feline. Sucked inward, her digits disappeared in divine waters. Just when her canal seemed to end, it expanded with wet desire. "Harder! More! More fingers!" the aroused photographer shouted.

Encouraged by shared lust, Haley went for broke. The brave girl added a fourth finger, finally wiggling an entire fist into her depths. Lifting her legs in a stirrup-like position, she cried out. Forgetting the photo shoot, any remaining vanity was abandoned.

Her vaginal canal swallowed the fist, inflaming every inch. Tightening thighs strained her g-spot like an overinflated balloon. Just when she reached her depths, the lair stretched even more, begging for an entire arm.

The camera snaps became white noise in her ears. Her only focus was how deep her fist would end up. *Will it come out my mouth?* She began to wonder. As she reached her forearm, Haley exploded, devouring the live limb inside her. Her thighs imprisoned her fist like an outlaw fetus.

That fact wasn't lost on Bruce. The girl's body was molded for breeding. Seeing the intensity upon the subject's face, he stopped. Although his job was to document every moment, there was no need to go further. *She's a breeder,* he assured himself. However, the rare decision wasn't his to make.

He remained silent, watching the strangulation of her fist. Her body shook, unable to stop the jolting spasms.

Bruce said, "We're done." His words fell on deaf ears, as the sensual redhead pumped away. One more orgasm shot through her cramped canal. He shouted again, "Haley! That's enough!"

The redhead snapped back to reality. Realizing what she'd done, her fist was forced from the cavern. Shaking her arm, the blood slowly returned. Pins and needles shot through her, only outdone by the waterfall cascading down her anal canyon.

"Was it good? I mean...was it great?" she asked.

He paused, searching his spent mind for accurate words. "In all my years doing this, you're the best I've ever photographed."

A glow filled Haley, having never been complimented so strongly. A stroke of guilt struck Bruce, realizing his truthful words assured her captivity. He quickly forced himself to detach. "Let me send these into my boss. Stay right there, I just need to send the files."

He grabbed the dress, hurrying into a side room.

"My dress! Why are you taking it?"

He didn't answer, disappearing inside.

Haley recovered, feeling the wet puddle beneath her. *Did I really just fist myself? I wonder if that's gonna end up on Facebook?* She sarcastically thought.

*****

Bruce uploaded the files onto his Internet phone. His shaking fingers typed away. After hitting send, he quickly dialed a number. "Mr. Cruz...I think we've got a breeder."

"That's not your decision to make. You should know better by now," the 40-year old, Victor Cruz scolded. "A decision of such consequence...is not made lightly."

"Absolutely, sir. I'm sorry to overstep. The files should arrive any moment."

There was a pause, as the downloaded files came into focus. "A redhead?" Victor asked.

"I know you called for a blond...but there's just something...exotic about this one. The pictures don't even do her justice."

"Did I complain?"

"No, sir."

"She'd be the first of her kind around here...well, at least since...never mind. Does she have any family?"

"From what I've gathered...*if* she has any at all...they don't know she's here. By the time any one asks...she'll be long gone," Bruce said.

"So you really believe she's more than just a prostitute?"

"I do," he said in truth.

Victor studied the images a bit longer. "Childbearing hips...nice vaginal depth. Ms. Haley White...I'll consider her. If not, she'll still be a nice addition to the stable. Abduct her. Make it quick and clean...no mess this time. Get her on my plane immediately, drugged for the flight. Good work, Mr. Knight."

"Sir, can I ask...is my time served yet? Ten loyal years at your side...should be enough to repay my mistake."

"*Enough*...is when I say so. Do you understand?" Victor asked.

"Yes, sir."

Without another word, Victor ended the connection.

Two strong men approached the seated man. They were part of a main guard, under Bruce Knight's authority. Tommy Johns had a shaved head, Rico Rains had buzzed brown hair. "Is it time?" Tommy asked.

"Yeah," Bruce said apprehensively. "Be gentle with this one...she's too valuable to lose."

"What if she puts up a fight?" one man asked, holding rope and a gag. "They always do."

Bruce opened a desk drawer, revealing a bottle and cloth. "You hold her down...I'll chloroform her into submission," he said, pouring a cap full into the rag. "It will keep her calm enough...to get her in the trunk."

*****

An apprehensive Bruce Knight exited the room, slowly approaching Haley with a rag. The nude girl slowly stood, unaware of her coming fate. "So, was I chosen?"

"You were," he said softly.

Her face lit up. "Cool! What happens next?"

Before he answered, Tommy and Rico's muscular frames appeared from behind. Her face darkened. A panicked Haley quickly covered herself up. "Who are they? What's happening?" she asked.

Tommy Johns warned, "You can either go gently...or not so gently. It's up to you," he said in a tough manner.

The frightened girl looked Bruce in the eyes. Her hurt matched the guilt in his own, forcing his stare away. "You lied to me!" Haley shouted.

"For your sake...cooperate," he warned her.

The two guards began their approach. Dropping her covering, vanity was suddenly bypassed for survival. Haley's heart pounded, heightening every sense inside her.

Right before they reached her, panic filled her brain, *Run. This is your last chance to escape.* The curvy redhead made a run for the door. Her soft, bare-feet scraped against the cement floor as her large breast bounced.

She ran with everything inside, nearing the exit. It appeared she was going to make it, when suddenly, a thick arm wrapped around her breasts. Lifted up, her momentum was stopped.

Her teardrop mounds were squashed against Rico's thick arms, inverting Haley's erect nipples. She tried to shout, as his hand cupped her mouth and nostrils. As her legs kicked outward, her round butt cheeks bounced against his hard cock. Nothing turned the guards on like a chase.

He carried her struggling body to the blanket, laying her down. Tommy pinned her ankles, as Rico held her wrists. The two drooled at the sight of the tearful, helpless girl. Mascara trickled down her face, as her soft body trembled before them. "Help me," she begged Bruce.

Knowing he had no choice, Mr. Knight approached her side. Running a hand through her soft hair, he tried to calm her. "This will make things a bit easier," he said, placing the moist rag over Haley's mouth and nose.

Her struggle intensified, holding her breath the entire time. "Mmmph..." she muffled through the rag.

Bruce tried to convince her. "Don't fight it...take deep breaths. The longer you wait, the more dangerous this is. You'll overdose," he warned, looking her in the eye.

Realizing he was speaking truth, she gave in. Her body tensed stiffly, as she obeyed. Bruce placed a hand in between the valley of breast meat, feeling her heart thump erratically. However, he searched for expanding lungs.

Haley inhaled deeply, as her body began to calm. After multiple deep breaths, all tension faded from her face. Her beautiful teal eyes started to roll, while the lids fluttered to stay open.

Vision began to blur, ranging between focal lengths. A moment of clear focus returned, as she used it for a last plea. Piercing Bruce's deep blue eyes with her helpless stare, he looked away again, powerless to grant her wish. In reality, his fate was as captive as hers.

After another inhalation, her eyes shut. She wasn't asleep, though in a twilight zone. Bruce removed the rag, returning her breath. As her mouth gaped open, another rag was stuffed deep inside, gagging her.

The two guards took charge, flipping her nude body over. Pulling her wrists behind her back, they were tightly tied with rope. After that, her ankles were crossed, bound as one.

"Not so tight," Bruce insisted, seeing the appendages swell with blue.

They rolled their eyes, loosening the binds. "What's gotten into you?" Tommy asked. "You never gave a damn before?"

"I already told you. She's valuable...to Victor," he said in annoyance.

"To Victor...or you?" he asked in jest, making Rico laugh.

A surge of anger filled Bruce, hating to be disrespected by subordinates. Removing his weapon, he aimed at the man's head. "Disrespect me again...I'll end you."

"I was just messing around...honestly," Tommy said in fear.

Returning the weapon to his side, he ordered, "We have a schedule to keep."

Pulling the drowsy redhead to her feet, Rico thrust the bound, curvy captive over his shoulder.

"Dizzy," Haley moaned, rushed into the back alley. A limo awaited her. The trunk was opened, as the drowsy girl was forced inside. "No," she begged, being claustrophobic. However, it didn't matter to her kidnappers, who slammed it shut.

Darkness filled her blurred vision, as Haley felt the car move. A part of her was thankful to still be drugged, keeping her calm. Slipping in and out of consciousness, she fought the restraints, rolling around the tight trunk. Feeling for something sharp to cut the binding, her weak arms found nothing. It finally hit her...there was no escape.

After thirty minutes, the chloroform started to wear off. Her panic increased in conjunction with sobriety. She kicked at the trunk, hoping someone would hear. The car finally stopped, trunk opened.

Unfortunately, it was Tommy Johns. Haley immediately thrust her bound ankles at him, which he caught. Lifting her upside down, she was thrust over his shoulder again.

Haley's first sight was concrete. She craned her head, discovering a lavish, private plane. The nude captive was ferried up a flight of mobile stairs, into the ritzy cabin. Once the door was sealed, she was moved to a sectioned room. Laid on the bed, the gag was yanked from her throat. She coughed up a sea of saliva. Pulled forward, her ties were cut free.

"Where are you taking me?" she shouted.

"To your new home," Tommy said. He looked toward Bruce, who watched from a distance. "She's ready for you."

Bruce approached. As petrified as Haley was, something about the photographer assured her safety. That quickly changed, as Mr.

Knight unleashed a hypodermic needle. Placing the spear in a liquid filled vile, he primed the plunger, filling it.

Seeing him do it, Haley shouted, "I don't like needles!"

As her body flailed again, the men held her down. "This will only hurt for a moment," Bruce assured her, swabbing her neck with an alcohol pad.

"Keep me safe," she begged him, staring deeply in his eyes.

He didn't verbally answer, though his returned gaze spoke volumes. Pressing the needle's spear against Haley's vein, he entered it. Forcing the plunger to its end, a large dose of medicine emptied into her body.

For the second time that night, the young woman was drugged to sleep. Her last thought was an acknowledgment of fate. She was being abducted overseas, no longer free. Haley White officially belonged to another. To whom and for what purpose, remained a mystery.

CHAPTER TWO

Haley bounced between the realm of consciousness and sleep, dreams and nightmares. She didn't know if the groping sensations were real or imagined. Of course, throughout the 3-hour flight, the feelings were real. The nude girl remained sprawled upon the bed, molested.

If Bruce hadn't stayed inside the room, she'd have been violated much worse. He allowed the men the usual right to roam, though demanded a new rule. *No intercourse.*

Upset at his sudden strictness, they accepted the new limitations. While Ms. White slept, their eager hands carved every inch of her curved body. Her nipples were feasted upon, along with her vaginal honey. Before they could kiss another set of lips, Bruce stopped them. "Don't kiss her! That right belongs to Mr. Cruz," he said. The men realized he was projecting his own desires.

Upon landing, Haley was carried to another car trunk, sealed inside. She wasn't awake yet, though could sense humid air. By the time she fully awokethe captive was in her new quarters.

"Help!" she shouted, awakening in a new reality. Bolting up inside a bunk bed, she still felt phantom hands roving her. Looking around, there were 20 nude girls watching from adjoining bunks. They were all different shapes and sizes, acquired to satisfy different tastes.

Each girl was exotic and beautiful. Most had dark hair, tanned skin. There were three blondes of British, Canadian, and Australian heritage, though no other Americans or redheads. As different as they all were, one commonality was shared: fear.

"Where am I? What is this place?" Haley asked.

The girls quickly turned away, already warned to remain quiet. Of course, they were as clueless as she was. A few of them didn't speak English, though their captor's cruelness translated perfectly.

Receiving a non-response, she looked around, studying the rows of beds. Although puzzled to its mysterious nature, Haley's questions would soon be answered.

Tommy and Rico entered the room, banging the edges of the bunk beds. "Up! On your feet, now!"

The girls exited the bunks, rising before they were *helped.* Lined up, they were led onto a large open stage. It was dark. They were pressed together like plywood. Haley's left arm brushed the soft skin of another, as a different girl's arm touched her right.

The guards backed up, shouting, "Turn them on!"

Two spotlights glared at the girls. Shielding their eyes, their pupils slowly adjusted. However, their sight wasn't important to the man behind the lights. All that mattered was his own.

A few more moments of quiet remained. Haley's sight returned. Looking across the stage, she was third in line. Shifting her focus, she spotted a dark haired man with olive skin. He wore a pinstriped suit with a blue necktie. Lust filled his eyes, as he paced the line of nudes.

His name was Victor Cruz, and power seeped from his skin. The man was an heir to an empire. He wasn't a regal lord, but a drug lord. Started generations before him, he was bequeathed a trillion-dollar drug and prostitution ring. In effect, it brought power beyond comprehension. His money insured his throne.

Victor constantly searched for a suitable breeder. Throughout his rule, there were only five worthy enough to produce his heir. They possessed the rare combination of exotic beauty, childbearing quality, and broken obedience. Unfortunately, they kept producing girls, an unacceptable choice to run his empire. However, even *they* served purpose.

As Ms. White trailed him with her eyes, she spotted Bruce nearby. The two connected gazes, quickly averting. After a brief visual study, Victor headed toward the girls.

Staring at the first victim, he pressed against her. Before doing anything, he violently sniffed. A cringe crossed his face, as he immediately dropped to his knees. The brown haired slave stiffened in fear. Spreading her lips wide, he brought his nose to her vaginal lair. After another strong inhalation, he turned his head away.

"This one's rotten. Toss it out...now!"

Rico grabbed the frightened girl by the arm, yanking her away. "No!" she cried, forced from the stage.

Next, Victor arrived at the second in line. He reached for the young captive's head. She was thin with raven black hair and dark eyes. Her ethnicity was South American, similar to his own. "Relajarse." He told her to relax, though she couldn't seem to.

His hand stroked her hair. Running his fingers through each strand, she calmed a bit. Continuing down her body, he trailed her skin, arriving at tiny A-cup breasts. Her dark aureoles were raised to their limits. Upon squeezing them, her knees buckled. She was virgin to any sexual act or touch.

Placing his hands at her side, he traced her nonexistent curves, noting a lack of childbearing quality. He turned her around, running his hand across her flat behind. Smacking her cheeks, they failed to answer back.

After bending her over, he knelt at her backside. The captive's eyes opened wide, as his thumbs parted her folds. She gasped as he searched for imperfections or disease. Leaning inward, his nose practically pierced her womanhood. Inhaling the deep scent, her tender flesh swayed in his natural wind.

Standing up, a guard approached. Victor Cruz turned to Tommy, saying only, "Sex slave."

The guard grabbed the virgin girl. She pulled away, crying out in a heavy accent, "No!" Understanding few English words, *slave* was one of them. Her struggle only lasted a moment, as Tommy seized her weak frame. Tossing her over his shoulder, she was carried out in tears.

Witnessing the act, Haley's heart pounded with worry. She'd seen enough TV to fear sex slavery's fate. Her adrenaline flowed. Although her rebellious side was only a defensive mechanism, it was about to kick in.

Victor Cruz paused at the sight of the curvaceous redhead. He dissected every inch with his hungry eyes. She was so different than his usual victim, so exotic to him. He stepped up to Haley, as she stiffened to stone. Touching her shiny red hair, he leaned in, sniffing. His hot breath against her neck sent chills throughout her body.

Placing his hands at her throat, he let them linger, sending a silent warning. The fight in her eyes was not welcome in such a place. After tightening a bit, he slowly moved down to her bulging breasts.

Tasting her engorged nipples, he sucked without mercy. Haley grunted from the dry-feeding's sting. The rhythm upon his lips emulated a drinking newborn, as his hands squeezed her breasts in powerful pulses.

Sucking until her nipple was raw with sensitivity, he forced himself away. His hands slid down the sides of her breasts, continuing onward. Arriving at her hips, he skied the heavenly slopes. Their borders stretched far and wide, redefining the term, *childbearing*.

Bruce watched from a distance, recognizing the look in his boss's eyes. The powerful man hungered like never before. Mr.

Knight knew his instinct was correct. *She'll be bred...I know it.* However, that decision was Victor's alone.

Kneeling downward, Mr. Cruz placed his thumbs on Haley's lips, sniffing inward. Shame filled her, refusing to let him penetrate. She thought to herself, *I'd rather die!*

Spreading her firm pinkness, the scent of royalty filled Victor's nostrils. He was suddenly awash in a bathtub of sweet rose petals. Although he personally forbids pleasure at that stage, he couldn't help but taste her.

Moving in, his mouth cupped her masterpiece. As contact was made, Haley yanked away. Bruce gasped, knowing such defiance was a death sentence. Victor turned angry, grabbing onto Haley's hips. He pulled her into his face, swallowing her full vaginal lips into his watering mouth. No one denied him, especially in front of others.

She gasped, continuing to pull away. Clipping her knees at the joints, he forced her to the ground. Her thighs were spread, as her hands were trapped inside his. Digging into her with his tongue, he pumped in a forceful pounding motion. The fearful girls turned their captive heads, watching him violate her orally. It was just a glimpse into their own futures.

His rhythmic thrusts continued, impaling her with a tense tongue. She continued to fight his grip, not matching his strength. The more she fought, the more her clit engorged. With each inward visit, his lips crashed into her swollen button.

Within minutes, her body quaked with lust. A hot sensation trickled through her like fuel of the highest octane. Rolling rain flooded Victor's mouth, as her legs were pinned still by his grasp.

She continued convulsing on the floor, side-eyed by her new sisters. Victor didn't stop until every drop was consumed. Finishing with her, he stood up, wiping his wet mouth. He shouted at the others. "No one denies my command!"

Rico joined him, as Mr. Cruz straightened his suit. "Where does this one go, sir?"

Victor paused. Bruce's heart thumped. Although neither outcome was pleasant, Mr. Knight knew that one was much worse than the other.

"Train her for sex slavery. I'll never let a disobedient whore carry my child. Let's see if her attitude changes after that."

"Yes, sir," Rico said, lifting the drained girl into a cradle carry. The frightened girl was removed, as Victor continued his inspections.

Bruce watched Haley closely, as she returned his concerned gaze. He knew her life was about to change, because he was tasked with changing it.

*****

Ten women survived the inspection process. The others disappeared, not seen again. No one was picked to breed. The new slaves occupied a shanty room with thin mattresses. That was their new home for a while. The moment Haley saw it, she thought, *Suddenly breeding doesn't sound so bad.*

Bruce Knight, Tommy Johns, and Rico Rains entered, joined by multiple guards. Victor Cruz followed behind, zeroing in on Haley. Seeing his challenging gaze, she turned away in anger. Bruce stepped up to the line of ten. "Choose a bed."

The scared girls headed for the nearest choice, reclining upon the cheap material. Mr. Knight walked across the room, inspecting each one. As he spoke, a translator followed him. "Life as you knew it...is over. Your dreams of professional modeling are dead. Now, you're all prostitutes for Mr. Victor Cruz. He is a powerful man...head of the largest drug and prostitution cartel in North America. Cross him and you'll die."

Haley watched in disbelief at her frightening future. *I hope this guy has an ounce of compassion.*

"Self-pleasure is no longer a word in your vocabulary. Everything you feel will be for your client. If he wants you to feel pleasure...you'll feel pleasure. If he wants you to feel pain...you'll feel pain. In most cases...he'll want the latter. However, before you work as a professional call girl...you'll learn the profession. Over the coming weeks, you'll be taught how to follow direction...and deliver pleasure. That all starts with discipline. Therefore, that's where we'll begin."

Gasps sounded from the girls, knowing discipline involved pain.

"The men behind me...will be the ones to break you." He turned to the men. "Gentlemen...choose your girl."

Each man hurried toward his favorite, as Bruce headed away from his choice. "Mr. Knight!" Victor called out. The group paused, staring back at him. "Train the redhead. She needs a firm hand."

He sighed, knowing his feelings would complicate matters. Nodding, he said, "Yes, sir."

Each man got his girl, as Bruce approached Haley. The stubborn girl looked away. "On your hands and knees," he said firmly.

"Fuck you," she shouted in anger.

Knowing Victor was watching, he couldn't reason with her. He whispered, "That man will have you killed. Do you want to die?"

She remained stubborn. Having no choice, Bruce forced her down to the mattress. His brute power shocked her, as he positioned her body into a doggy-style form. Her round behind was in prime position, exposing her hanging red lips.

"Asshole," she said.

"Deal with her insubordination," Victor demanded.

Bruce stood, taking a deep breath. He didn't want to hurt her, though if she weren't broken by training's completion, her fate would be worse than spankings.

He prepared his hand, giving her a medium smack upon her cheek.

"My foster-father hit harder than that," she challenged. Following up, the next was much harder. Each smack was harder than the last. With each blow, the sting increased. Biting her lip, the stubborn girl fought from breaking. The sound of crackling skin echoed through the air, reddening each captive.

As an hour of spent spankings passed, some of the girls began to break. Cries filled the room. However, Haley held back her tears…at least on the outside.

After two hours, her behind was covered in a deep red hue. Bruce's hand began to hurt, as he thought to himself, *Please break...don't make me do something worse.*

Victor stepped up, stopping the process. "That's enough for today. We'll continue again tomorrow."

The next day arrived, as the spankings continued. More of the girls broke down, begging, "Please, I'll do anything...just stop!" Afterward, they were made to watch Haley, endure three more hours of harsh spankings. Exhaustion filled Bruce's face.

Victor approached again, shaking his head in disappointment. "I've never seen one hold out this long."

"What next? She's close...but stubborn." Mr. Knight inquired.

Mr. Cruz paused for a moment, as his eyes filled with excitement. "Use the belt."

Bruce and Haley simultaneously shuddered. However, the stubborn redhead still remained headstrong.

Removing his leather strap, Ms. White tensed, remaining in position. Bruce leaned in, whispering, "Whatever you're hanging on to...can't be worth your life."

Victor interrupted, "Are we ready?"

"Yeah," he said, tightening his grip upon the belt. He repeated a statement all the girls were told, "By breaking, you're officially signing a contract. At that moment, you surrender your body to us. Give in now...and avoid the pain."

She didn't make a sound.

His reluctant arm went backward, flung towards Haley's bottom. The first lash crossed her bountiful buns. "Ouch!" she shouted, as shock took over. Emotions she had never felt before filled her. It was definitely pain, though something else was present.

Another leather spanking was administered, causing chills to fill her naked skin. She trembled, overcome by a mysterious force. As each whipping was administered, the feeling grew more intense. Her thighs tightened in anticipation, almost excited for the next blow.

What's wrong with you? She chastised herself, tearing from the punishment. The high level of pain uncorked a guarded lust. It was a force unable to be tapped by a simple hand spanking. Unlocked from the dungeons of her mind, it was unleashed tenfold. As the fifth lashing crossed her pear-shaped bottom, she cried out. Tears fell from her eyes, competing with drops of a vaginal nature.

Bruce froze in disbelief, mesmerized by Haley's raw spasms. His guilt slightly dulled, having never witnessed a slave cum at such treatment. He suddenly discovered her true nature wasn't dominant, after all.

"Harder," Mr. Cruz ordered, erect beyond pleasure.

Another hard lash crossed Haley's bottom. She dropped down to the bed, exploding in stinging lust. Tightening every muscle, her body writhed upon the mattress. Spreading her legs, she squashed her clit into the rough cloth.

The whippings continued throughout, pushing her to the edge of humanity. Like a finale at a fireworks display, pops of fire danced around her head. Streams of vaginal rain cooled her orgasm, leaving suds of stickiness upon her lips.

Bruce went to flog her again, as Victor's hand stopped him. Together they witnessed her official breaking. As the orgasm subsided, an ocean of tears poured from Haley's shamed eyes. Bruce shattered a surface once cracked by her foster-father. "I belong to you," she cried out, able to take no more. The pent up pain flowed like acid rain.

The sound of tearful capitulation was like the richest music to Victor's ears. His erection reached its maximum height.

Bruce exhaled, thankful it was over. "She's broken."

Victor shook his head. "You know better than that. The first submission is what *they* want to tell you. The following one...is what *you* want to hear," he said.

"You doubt her tears?" he asked.

A look of displeasure crossed Victor's face. Bruce had never questioned his authority, especially in front of slaves. "Do you dare question my expertise?"

"No sir," he assured, quickly remembering his place. "Back on your hands and knees," he ordered Haley.

The tearful girl returned to her position, flogged another five times. As horrible as it seemed, her masochistic side craved the burning sting again. She didn't realize it, though it wasn't pain that unleashed her pleasure. It was something deeper.

For the first time in her life, Haley truly let go of control. No longer on guard, she accepted a fate of giving herself to others. It went against everything she once pretended to be, though her submissive nature finally claimed her. The many masks of the past were lifted, exposing her soul.

After the sessions, nurses administered cold compresses upon red skin. Bedridden for a few days, Haley emptied of tears. More importantly to Victor, she'd also emptied of freewill. All the girls came to accept their daily spankings, beginning to crave them. It was as if their stolen self-worth was replaced.

In a mere week's time, the naive girls were ready to be reprogrammed. Thoughts of escape disappeared. The only thing in Haley's mind was, *What will they do next? When will they ask me to please them again, therefore bringing me rare pleasure?*

Bruce trembled in his bed after the belt punishment. It was the only place safe from spying eyes; the only place safe to feel emotion. Years of repressed guilt had taken its toll, making him momentarily consider suicide. However, he'd just be replaced by another. Haley would be worse off for it.

The last day of the week, Victor approached a nude, healed Haley. "On your hands and knees," he ordered.

Emulating a robot, the redhead immediately got into position. He began laughing, letting his voice echo off the walls. "Tell me, slave. Would you like the hand...or the belt?" he asked in a wicked way.

A long pause came from Haley, as if she was embarrassed to admit it. Everyone thought they knew what she'd say. They were wrong.

"The belt," she said, shocking Bruce.

A big smile crossed Victor's face. "Step one is complete. Sexual training begins tomorrow," he said, walking away.

"Should I beat her?" Bruce asked.

Victor paused. "She wants it...so, no. Slaves don't get what they want. They get what I want them to have."

Mr. Knight returned his attention to Haley. *Why can't I detach from this girl? Why do I care so much about her? She's nothing to me.* Though deep in his heart, he knew why. Even if his head refused to acknowledge it.

CHAPTER THREE

Having been broken, the sexual training phase began. During their idle captivity, the slaves remained chained, not permitted to speak. Fed sparsely for the first week, they thirsted and hungered. It was a way of forcing them to adapt. When the food and water finally arrived, they were greatly appreciative. Many thanked the guards on their hands and knees. Stockholm Syndrome was setting in.

Although the discipline training only lasted seven days, the harsh punishment managed to break them of their freewill. No complaints were heard, even from Haley. Of course, it was easier for her, having no ties to her old life.

Her brain went into survival mode, abandoning all thoughts of personal want. Instead, she focused on life's bare necessities, awaiting Victor's next command. At that point, it was her only sense of worth.

Their outer bruises healed, only remaining inside. The girls were unchained, standing nude at the edge of their mattresses. Each guard stood before their assigned slave.

Bruce Knight stepped up, joined by an eager Victor Cruz. Mr. Knight addressed the group. "Now that you know the consequences of freewill, it's time to train you sexually. As I told you before, your pleasure is not important. Your existence is merely to please the clients...nothing more. We'll begin with oral."

The girls stared straight ahead, knowing better than to show displeasure. Bruce took his spot in front of Haley. He refused to gaze into her eyes, knowing a sex slave would only stare back. Even if the transition weren't complete, it wouldn't be the warmth he helped extinguish.

"Open your mouths!" Bruce ordered the girls.

Each one obeyed, opening their mouths wide. Bruce stuck his extended finger to the back of Haley's tongue. Beauty soured from the redhead's face, as she gagged forcefully.

Each guard commenced with their slaves, creating a concert of forced gagging. Their fingers were not quite as gentle. Haley White tried to pull away, though Bruce's strong arm held her head in place. "Relax the back of your tongue."

The gagging fit continued, as her fear took over. A river of saliva sailed from her mouth. It appeared she was going to lose control like a few of her nearby sisters. Bruce finally connected eyes with Haley, forcing her to connect back. "Focus on me," he said. "Let your tongue go limp."

The curvy redhead zoned in on his deep blue eyes. Getting lost in them, she was suddenly able to focus on his instruction. Her tongue fully relaxed, calming her gagging. "Good girl," he rewarded her.

However, the prize was a deeper journey into an uncharted throat. An even more intense purging began, taking her to the limits. He trapped her in-place for a few moments. "Focus on me again," he said, gazing into her eyes. "Relax your throat. In fact, relax every muscle in your body. Don't fight the pressure, embrace it."

A last major gag sounded from her, spilling another river of saliva. By that time, an ocean of her sweetness filled the floor. Having no choice, she forced her throat muscles to relax.

Tears streamed her face, as she returned to calmness. "Good girl," he assured her again. Removing his finger, Haley swallowed. Having lost so much saliva, she needed to wet her throat. She didn't realize it would soon be wet with another fluid.

As Haley wiped the tears from her eyes, she was led to her knees. The girl's vision cleared, seeing a nine-inch cock headed her way. Bruce pried Haley's mouth open, aiming his bulbous head into her primed mouth.

Her teeth slightly chafed his skin, forcing him to pry her jaw wider. She'd never had oral sex before. Though, even if she had, Bruce's unmatched girth and length put others to shame.

The veiny offering fought its way across her sensitive tongue. As it went deeper, she began to gag again. "Remember what I taught you. Just because it's bigger, the process doesn't change.

Calming her glands, she shut her eyes, filled with his manly offering. The spear arrived at her throat, plugging her airway. She momentarily struggled for breath, as he ordered her, "Hold your breath."

Obeying, she let it rest over her air hole. Feeling enough time pass, Mr. Knight freed the human plug. He began to pump her mouth, keeping ahold of her teeth and jaw. "These men won't put up with bad blow-jobs. *Never*...I mean, *never* use teeth."

Releasing his hold, he decided to test her. Following his instruction, she strained her jaw, pushing it to its limits. "Tighten the lips only," he ordered. Her pillowy lips gripped his wide invader. Firing his missile in and out, he gripped her red hair. Using it to control her rhythm, he increased her speed to a feverish rate.

The forced thrusts continued. Just when it appeared his pipe couldn't penetrate any deeper, he speared it deeper into her throat. After a deep gag, she refocused her newfound skills. Not missing a beat, she continued. Bruce was impressed, marveling at the quick learner.

As her saliva poured down his shaft, hot cum crawled up his pleasure ladder. His bouncing balls were completely coated, increasing the sensation. He addressed her before losing control, "Feel my load begin to approach. Use your lips to locate the sudden swelling within...so you don't choke on it." His face tensed, as the grip upon her hair tightened. She grimaced, lost in his fury.

He looked down at her, seeing her teal eyes stare up at him. An ounce of innocence remained, ready to be ruined by another forbidden act. "Prepare your throat," he shouted. A sweet coating flooded her mouth, unleashing his marshmallow cream.

Spurts of semen rushed into her throat. The foreign feeling made her gag, as she hadn't intended to swallow. Though, the salty assault didn't offer her a choice. It smoothly flowed into her stomach.

Grunting into the air, he tightened every muscle in his body. He nearly tore Haley's hair at the root, as her lips milked him in intense motion. His heavy cum continued spraying her mouth, covering his rod with every outward thrust.

Holding her still, he emptied the last of himself. "Let your taste-buds recognize my flavor...each man will be different, yet familiar. In time, you must come to crave this...since it will be a meal you have often."

She followed his advice, holding some in her mouth as he withdrew. Soaking his seed into her senses, Haley savored every drop. Once afraid of the act, she quickly embraced it.

"Good girl," Bruce said, holding her face, connecting with her eyes again. "You can finish it now." The gorgeous redhead swallowed the remainder, sticking out her clean tongue afterward. It was clear she wanted to please him.

He placed a hand on her face, rubbing her soft cheek. The loving act confused her, also confusing himself.

Witnessing the compassion, Victor's internal alarm sounded. Between Bruce's questioning of her beatings, and the odd act of softness, he was starting to doubt his man's fortitude. "How'd she do?" Victor's voice interrupted the moment.

A startled Bruce quickly ended the kind gesture, yanking his pants up. "Acceptable," he said, trying not to show his elation.

"For her sake, it's a lucky thing she has another week to learn."

*****

After a full week of constant blowjobs, sperm swallowing, and forced facials, she passed the test. The next lesson was anal sex. Since sensual, vaginal penetration was the least requested menu item, it was saved for last.

In the waiting period, constant boredom claimed the captives' lives. Haley's craving for each sexual act grew each day. It became her reason for existing, sole purpose.

Pleased to see the next phase, she arrived at an unpleasant reality. Two girls were missing. They failed the blowjob test, continuously using teeth. Needless to say, the group got a new incentive to succeed.

Bruce Knight went to take his spot, when Victor's hand stopped him. "Today...there will be a change."

"Change?"

"For this job, I think Rico is more suited."

"Why?"

"I have my reasons. Take your place at the thin virgin."

A look of sickness filled Bruce's face. He stared over at Haley, who was awaiting his arrival. Instead, Rico claimed his place. The subordinate guard stared Bruce down, taunting him with licked lips.

Looking away, Mr. Knight arrived at the thin, South American virgin. She lay flat upon the mattress, emulating the other girls. Unlike Haley, fear still claimed her eyes.

"Begin!" Bruce announced in a disappointed voice. He removed his clothes, along with the rest of the guards. Each one bulged with muscles, forced to train daily.

He knelt upon the bed, spreading the thin girl's legs. Licking his hand, he massaged her soft anal tissue. Taking his time, he lubed the sphincter, slowly wiggling a finger inside her hidden hole. As expected, she tightened further.

Next, he added a second finger, causing her to tense more. Working the appendages in a pumping rhythm, he slowly primed her for a larger guest. The compassion he displayed further disturbed Victor. Bruce was once aggressive, angry. He took that anger out on the slaves.

He had suddenly softened. The roots of compassion arrived with Haley, though that wasn't obvious to Victor yet. However, since the feisty redhead needed to be fully broken, Bruce clearly wasn't trusted with the rough lesson.

After withdrawing his fingers, Bruce placed the dome-shaped cock head at the virgin's hole. Before entering, he gazed over at Haley. She wasn't afforded the same care.

Rico stretched her cheeks open. He let a glob of saliva seep down her vaginal highway, pooling in her bronze eye. With no stretching afforded her, Rico aimed directly for the bullseye. Haley's legs were lifted into a stirrup position. The aggressive guard's eight-inch cock forced its way through the tight anal ring.

Haley moaned, as her hands gripped the mattress's edge. With one strong thrust, Rico was fully buried inside her. Her feet rested upon his shoulders, tense and twisted. Grabbing her by the thighs, he pulled her closer into him, forcing his rod even deeper.

The slave bit her bottom lip, as her long fingernails cut into the cheap cloth. Rico quickly pumped her, disallowing her sphincter to adapt. Every anal nerve was immediately stimulated, setting her tender canal ablaze with fire. *Don't go to the bathroom,* she silently begged herself. The phantom sensations confused her senses.

She shook uncontrollably, never pushed so far. The beatings were nothing compared to the anal experience. Her brain fought to decipher the difference between pleasure and pain. It failed to find the line.

Seeing the devouring of his desire, Bruce turned away. He eased his nine-inch cock inside the South American slave. She cried out, immediately choking his rod with her constricted hole.

Tears filled her eyes. To calm her, Mr. Knight began rubbing her clit. She suddenly softened, as the pleasure neared the pain. His thumb pressed downward on her fleshy button, spinning in slow, sensual circles.

Her moans increased, as anal restriction began to ease, allowing him deeper access. Moving inside, his bulbous cock claimed more territory. He gripped hold of her dark nipples. Pulling them outward, her A-cup breasts stretched with them.

The combined stimulations increased his slave's intensity. The overwhelming emotions began to make her cry. Seeing it, Bruce began taking small, quick breaths, causing her to emulate his action.

For the first time, he saw the look of pleasure begin to form. He knew she wouldn't orgasm from her first time, but at least she'd feel some pleasure.

The South American's moans were deafened by a different slave's lusty cry. It was Haley's. Her aggressive captor picked up pace, delivering an anal invasion. As the redhead's feet wrapped around Rico's neck, they nearly strangled him. She was about to meet the same fate.

Victor stepped up, shouting, "Begin erotic asphyxiation."

Haley's strained eyelids popped open in shock. She looked over at Bruce, who refused to stare back. It suddenly made sense to her. *That's why he was chosen for someone else. He wouldn't have done it to me.*

Ms. White was correct in her thinking. Mr. Knight wouldn't have completed the task. Victor knew that Rico would. The risky act was the most expensive fetish on the menu. It was also the most requested. If the slaves weren't properly trained, they'd suffocate, costing Mr. Cruz money.

Rico's callused hands were wrapped around Haley's tender throat. He squeezed her airway, as hard as her sphincter squeezed his cock. The tighter his grip, the more pleasure he received.

Victor announced loudly, making sure the shocked girls heard his instruction. "You will not fight the act...no, you will each embrace it. Don't try to breathe, simply drift into darkness."

Bruce wrapped his large hands around his slave's throat. The young girl tried to fight it, more than the others. Noticing it, Mr. Knight said to her, "Accept it! Go with it!" He realized she didn't understand. Thinking what to do, he said, "Sleep," following with a snoring sound.

Understanding the universal message, she shut her eyes, letting them roll back. As the oxygen escaped her, she allowed the sleeping process to begin. Watching her drift, he quickly turned toward Haley.

Rico pounded her dark cavern harder than before. He squeezed equally as hard. Staring over at Bruce, he unleashed a taunting smile. Mr. Knight wanted to leap at him, choking him in return. That was not an option.

Following Victor's instruction, Haley didn't fight the dizziness. Suddenly, the anal sensation merged with the sparks inside her head. The tighter he choked her, the deeper he sank inside. As his cock reached its base, she was stretched to the max. Her breasts stiffened, forcefully shaken with each banging.

Chills rose from every pore, as tiny pops of color flashed upon her inner lids. Right before passing out, she exploded into a violent orgasm, convulsing like an epileptic. Her body nearly levitated.

In reality, the act compressed her carotid arteries, blocking oxygen-rich blood to the brain. As the oxygen decreased, carbon dioxide increased. A rush of untamable sexual pleasure electrified her.

Feeling Haley's thick ass asphyxiate his cock, Rico grunted. He filled her forbidden flume with streams of seed. Her last memory before unconsciousness was DNA seeping into her undiscovered depths. Finally, her limp body gave in, passing out.

Bruce soiled his own slave's behind, as she also lost consciousness. He immediately released the grip upon her neck. The air was quickly returned, continuing the breathing process. She slept peacefully. Quickly returning his gaze to Haley, he witnessed a disturbing sight.

Rico continued to choke his victim, attempting to cum again. "No!" Bruce yelled, yanking his cock from his slave, rushing towards Rico. Seeing his challenger arrive, the guard also disconnected, restoring Haley's breath.

Bruce sideswiped his opponent to the floor, thrusting a fist into Rico's face. The treasonous move further confirmed Victor's suspicion. *He's gone soft.* Although the act was typically a death sentence, there was still use for him. There was a way to turn his compassion into an asset, if necessary. If not, he'd officially become expendable.

Tommy Johns pulled Bruce off, flinging his nude body to the floor. Rico was knocked unconscious, bloodied to a pulp.

Leaning into Bruce, Victor said, "Do you remember what I once told you? Emotions...will get you killed around here. Consider that your last warning."

He exited the room.

*****

That night, Bruce crept into the dark, sex slave quarters. A small sliver of moonlight penetrated the roof's skylight. The lunar body was perfectly positioned, highlighting Haley's face.

He crept to the edge of her bed, studying the cuffs around her wrists. Chains were linked to the wall, keeping the captives in place. Her heaving chest comforted his worries. Since he wasn't present for her recovery, there was no way of knowing if she had survived.

New thoughts plagued his mind. Picturing her future prostitution enraged him, knowing such animalistic acts would occur daily. *She'd be better off dead,* he told himself. A sickness filled his stomach, making him quickly exit the room. While he headed to purge himself in a toilet, Haley awakened.

Feeling a caring presence, she witnessed a faint glimpse of him closing the door. She almost wondered if it was a dream. The thoroughly exhausted girl shut her eyes again, drifting back to sleep. *It was just a dream,* she told herself in disappointment. A small part of her hoped he cared.

Chapter Four

After two weeks of anal and asphyxiation training, the final lesson was upon them. Although vaginal intercourse wasn't as popular, it was only below choking in monetary expense. The act was a loving one, which required the girls to fake a powerful emotion.

Only kissing surpassed coitus in sensuality, though that was banned years ago. Allured by the passionate act, clients often fell in love with the girls, unable to break the bond formed between the two. It never ended well.

As the current slaves were unchained from their cuffs, they awaited their next instruction. Even as broken in as Haley was, her nerves still jittered. After experiencing such intensity the week before, there was no ground left to tread. At least, she hoped not.

A sigh of relief exited her, as Bruce made the announcement. "Today...we'll start vaginal intercourse training. We'll work on technique and vaginal muscle control. Though, before all that...we'll start with seduction. Your main job with this...is to make these millionaire clients feel like a billion bucks. Each one of them will feel...as if they're the only one you care to please. No one else. Begin," he ordered, heading toward the South American slave.

Victor stopped him again, saying, "For this exercise...you'll return to the redhead."

A rare light encompassed Bruce's face. "Thank you...for trusting in me again."

Mr. Cruz nodded, looking over at Rico's busted face. It further reminded the drug lord of Bruce's inner weakness. Though for the current lesson, it worked to his advantage. The injured guard took his spot at the virgin slave.

Mr. Knight returned Haley. A smile crossed her face, though she quickly wiped it away. Such emotion wasn't permitted.

Each man instructed his own slave. Bruce addressed Haley, "You'll welcome the client by asking, 'how may I serve you, master?' Give it a try."

"How may I serve you, master?" she repeated in a flat tone.

"The words come out...though without emotion, they're meaningless. My advice is to think of someone...anyone you have feelings for. It could be an ex-boyfriend, or someone who just cares about you. Tap into that emotion. Look in my eyes...pretend you mean it. Make me believe it!"

Haley followed orders, gazing into his deep blue eyes. She tapped into truth, knowing Rico's beating was for her care. For a moment everything around her vanished. All thoughts of beatings, slavery, and fear faded into oblivion.

Her mouth opened, letting the words float like high butterflies. "How may I *serve* you, *master*?" The tone was softer than cotton balls, sweeter than sugar dipped chocolate. She quickly snapped from her trance, returning to reality. "Was that good enough?"

Bruce was forced from his own trance of teal, reminding himself that it was fake. "Perfect. I'd never know you were faking." The two remained silent, realizing the other girls were already in motion. "Next, tell me to take off my clothes, lie down, and get comfortable."

"Take off your clothes, lie down, and get comfortable," she repeated stiffly.

"Again...more passion. You *need* this man...or woman sexually. You *desire* them like nothing else in your life. If it helps...convince yourself they're the only ones left in your world...who you believe in."

Haley paused, letting her thought process begin again. *He doesn't even realize, he's describing himself. He's the closest thing to hope that I have.* Haley tapped into her heart. *How do I show my belief in him? How can I show him, he truly is the only one left in my world?* In a daring action, she moved in towards his lips.

Right before making contact, a voice sounded, "No!" Victor charged over, as Bruce pulled away. "Never, never, never...kiss a client! Never! I thought that was clear...apparently not! Do you understand me...slave?" Mr. Cruz yelled.

"Yes...I...I'm sorry."

"One sorry is all you get. Continue on," he said, stepping back to observe.

Following her initial request, Bruce removed his clothes and sprawled upon the bed. The nude redhead approached him awkwardly. Not knowing what to do, she straddled his cock.

"Hold it," he said, pausing her in mid-flight.

She stood up, "Did I do something wrong?"

"No. It's what you didn't do. Romance me, tease me...remember sensuality. The men who buy this service want to believe! They're not purchasing a prostitute...they're lying down with a girlfriend...a wife!"

Haley nodded, taking a deep breath. She was clearly stressed out by the deep task.

Bruce leaned up, embracing her hips. "Forget what I just said. Just do what comes natural. Pretend there's no client, no slavery...no money involved. We're just two people...in love. Can you try that?"

She nodded. He handed her a condom, officially leaving the rest in her hands. Blocking out the sexual moans from the other slaves, she focused on her partner. It was suddenly just her and Bruce. They never met in an abandoned warehouse. Their relationship wasn't one of forced abduction. It was a date in a happy, safe reality.

Haley slowly sat beside the muscular man. She touched his stubbled face, gazing into his eyes again. Running her red, lengthy nails down his chin, she tickled his throat.

Continuing through his chest hair, she circled his small, manly bumps, twisting and teasing his nipples. The tough man gasped, having never felt that before. Continuing onward, she traced the defined lines of his six-pack stomach.

Moving down, she arrived at his trimmed pubic hair. Bruce's cock was stone solid, as thick and long as ever before. Nearly touching it, she avoided any contact, keeping him on edge.

Tracing the edges of his phallus, she outlined the curved testicles, easing underneath them. Taking the steely marbles into her soft hands, she lifted them. Her tongue licked the patch of skin below, making him tense with pure pleasure.

Tickling the outer casing of his prostate, her moist flickers penetrated his dermal wall. Spreading his anal cheeks, she slowly sank downward, teasing the rim of his manly anus. The sexually experienced man suddenly shuddered, realizing there was more to learn.

Rising back upward, she pulled his balls higher. Wetting a trail through the middle, Haley parted the two dumplings at the seam. They split apart, as Ms. White spanned his globe. She swallowed his large sack inside her warm mouth, sucking both testes at once.

Freeing his swollen balls, Haley arrived at the base of Bruce's shaft. Keeping hold of his testes, she massaged them in one hand, stroking the 9-inch spear with the other. Climbing the risen ridge with her tongue, his urethra was primed. By the time his sensitive upper glands were soaked, she licked the meatus slit. The oozing pre-cum was cleaned from the head.

Exiting the penis, she licked a return trail upward. The slicked soaker hiked the trail of paradise in reverse. Sliding over his bellybutton, past his diaphragm, and across his throat, she ended at his chin. Finally face-to-face, Haley hung over him. A moment of silence spoke for them, tempted by each other's kiss again. "Did *that* make a believer out of you?"

He tried to find the words, saying, "Uhh...*yeah*."

She took the initiative, fully claiming the mantle of teacher. To protect her valuable womb from pregnancy, she slid the condom over his endless pole. Next, she straddled the anxious cock. "If you believed that...then you'll definitely believe this," she said, gripping the slicked head. Positioning it at her delicate crepe, she squatted upon it, engulfing it halfway inside.

A joint gasp exited both their lungs. Haley's pillows slowly swallowed the tower of ivory, encased like a grand sausage. He could feel her flowery fluff tug at the thin sheath of rubber, begging to taste her flesh. Placing her soft hands upon his bulging chest, she rode him in a rodeo of sensuality.

Her curved cheeks spread as she elevated upon his manhood, crimping closed while falling to the base of his balls. As beastly guards serenaded them with animalistic snorts and grunts, the two danced in a prom of their own. All that was missing was music, lights, and obnoxious teens in rental suits.

It was the most intense feeling she'd ever felt. Bruce had the feeling once before, years ago. Abandoning all thoughts from his mind, he had no intention of revisiting that moment.

Victor gazed around at the different speeds and deeds. All of them confirmed what he expected, *Nothing but whores.* However, as he came upon Haley's swanlike form, those thoughts disappeared. Her back was arched, feminine feet tucked into Bruce's hind thighs.

She bared the grace of Aphrodite, radiance of a rainbow. It was the ingredient he searched for in a breeder: perfection. Already having the beauty and learned-obedience, she finally achieved the motherly essence, which couldn't be taught. It was an untrainable quality.

He lost himself in their lovemaking, failing to recognize Bruce's role in it. Having only ever loved himself, Victor remained ignorant that two souls were required to ignite such passion. Mr. Knight was lucky for that oversight.

Suddenly, Bruce grabbed hold of Haley's round hips, pulling her down into him. His cock dug its way deeper into her, trying to drown in her wine. Instead, it would settle for spewing syrup inside the confines of a condom.

With every blast, he pushed her further down, impaling her soul. Phantom feelings entered her stomach, as if his cock crawled inside. Right as he emptied, Haley's spot was hit. She cried out, gripping a handful of his dark chest hair.

Her hips spun in small circles, as her white teeth nibbled her bottom lip. The moans echoed through the room, putting the other slaves to shame. All other acts ended, as all eyes turned to the entrancing show before them.

Together, the two let their joint flame simmer. Ms. White's head crashed upon Bruce's sweaty chest, collapsing in the heat of sensuality. Mr. Knight gripped Haley's curvy body in his strong embrace, running his hands along every familiar inch. His cock slowly sank to its flaccid state, covered in rubbery sweet pudding.

The redhead settled inside his arms, basking in the faux afterglow. They were suddenly interrupted by clapping. Opening their eyes, they were thrust from their world of fantasy. Looking around, reality hijacked their moment.

To their shock, the cheering came from Victor. He announced to the group, "*That*...slaves...is how to fake sensuality! That's how it's done. And that's...what I expect to see when your number's called. We're done for today."

As he left the room, Bruce and Haley's gaze returned. A week of sensual bliss flew by, each episode increasing in temperature. Upon the last act, they didn't speak a single word, realizing their fates would soon part. The shared moment of passion would be their last.

*****

Victor was in his plush office, finalizing the details of the next human shipment. A knock sounded upon the door. "Bruce, come in."

Mr. Knight entered, as stress tainted his face. "I need to talk to you."

Recognizing the serious tone, Mr. Cruz placed his pen to the desk's surface. "Then talk."

Nervousness overcame Bruce, an unusual trait for the tough man. "I need to ask something."

"Ask already! I'm busy...you know my time is money. Quit wasting both of them."

"I need to know...when will I be free?"

"We already discussed this...when I no longer need you."

"I've sacrificed everything for you...my home, my family, my principles."

"And we both know they never missed you back. I'm all you have. The Bruce Knight of the past died long ago...you've got nothing there."

"I've got nothing here."

"Nothing? I've sheltered, fed, and clothed you. Do you forget that I gave you the biggest gift of all?"

Bruce nodded. "I didn't forget."

"You're alive because of me...you ungrateful shit! Do you know how many other men were executed for doing what you did?"

"I've always wanted to know...why? Why not me? What did you see in me...to spare my life?"

Victor paused. "You really want to know?"

"I do."

"Physical strength...mental weakness. You were broken...yet capable."

"Of?"

"Power. It's why I made you my right-hand. That untapped potential...is the man you are today. I made you...therefore, I own you. The truth is, I haven't seen such vulnerable worth...someone so intriguing until...recently."

Bruce had stopped listening after the word weakness. "Be brutally honest with me. Will I be here for the rest of my life?"

Again Victor paused, weighing the value of truth. "You'll be here until I no longer need you." Of course, he didn't go into further detail.

Mr. Knight dropped his head in disappointment. It was as if his last reason for living was shattered. Though inside his heart, he knew one of those reasons was long gone. The other reason was on her way. He had officially given up on life. "Thanks for your honesty," he said, standing to exit.

Noting his depressed state, Victor decided it was time to use Bruce's newfound compassion to his advantage. "Before you leave...I have a task for you."

"Tell me...it'll be done."

"For this...I need to show you."

*****

Victor led Bruce to the line of sex slaves. Having finished their training, the nude women awaited their next journey. As Mr. Knight arrived, he studied the blank looks upon their faces. All emotion was gone.

However, one girl still had a hint of life. Last in line, Haley White side-eyed him. Although he enjoyed seeing her one last time, a part of him wished he hadn't. It only reminded him what he was losing.

Mr. Cruz addressed the girls. "Prepare to embark upon an exciting journey. By day's end, you'll be in Paraíso...or Paradise, to English ears. It's my world-famous brothel, located in Venezuela. Your servitude will begin soon. Having arrived useless, you leave here with new purpose. That purpose? Making me money. Just remember one last thing. Your one selfish act...will be your last."

The girls were marched toward the room's exit, as Bruce addressed Victor. "Why did you need me here?"

As Haley approached the door, Victor reached out, stopping her in place. A look of shock filled her, emulating Bruce's reaction. She remained silent, wondering, *Am I going to die?*

As the line disappeared, the door was closed. "You were correct in your initial assessment. Ms. White is more than just another sex slave...much more. She will birth the heir to my empire. I have no doubt...this one will be a boy. In fact, I demand it."

"If not?"

"Do I really need to spell that out?"

"No."

"I've been failed five times...all girls. I'm getting too old to wait."

"I still don't understand…what does this have to do with me?"

"You discovered her, therefore you're now in charge of protecting her. Such a tempting asset will be prime fucking material for the guards. They are not to lay a hand on her...understand? I'll hold you personally responsible if they do."

"I won't let you down, sir."

"I believe that," he said, turning away.

"Should I take her to a breeding suite?" Bruce asked.

"No. First...she must pass a medical exam, assuring her female parts are functioning correctly. Take Ms. Haley White to our doctor."

Part Two

Chosen to Breed

CHAPTER FIVE

The curvy redhead rode Bruce Knight like a stallion. Every muscle bulged on the tense man, as he struggled to withhold his flowing desire. For a moment, his gaze exited hers, studying a mirrored ceiling. It was like his soul escaped, hovering above the two lovers.

Such a unique perspective offered a captivating view. Red hair flew in the air-conditioned breeze, dancing in an unnatural wind. A feminine hourglass redefined itself with each movement. Some curves were added, while others were absorbed within.

She bounced upon his veiny offering, enacting her Kegel exercises. With each landing her hole tightened more. Her round cheeks milked Bruce's udder like a veteran farmer. Crescent-shaped hips were enhanced in the glassy reflection, stretching to infinity.

A rich hue filled the room. Golden light electrified gold-plated walls, adding a queenly glow to pale skin. High-end furnishings decorated the space, featuring marble floors, Persian rugs, antique trinkets, and leather couches. If it wasn't for a spilled bottle of Champagne and a scattered cocaine-line, it could've been mistaken for a Pharaoh's raided tomb.

The femme fatale withdrew Bruce's cock from her vagina, expertly guiding it into her hind hole of ill repute. Relaxing her sphincter like a true professional, she lowered herself without pause. Anal was her specialty.

Bruce gasped. His lover crashed down to the base of his cock, almost swallowing his balls. The force pushed them deeper into the cottony mattress. Lambskin sheets massaged their skin, cushioning the muscular man's bottom.

Feminine feet were set upon Bruce's broad chest, as the painted lady reached back for his knees. She lifted herself into a crab-crawl, arching her curves. The position intensified a merciless anal grip.

Mr. Knight's cock stiffened into a solid state. Like a performer in a lustful circus, the redhead's body bounced like a trampoline of anal acrobatics. Bruce grimaced his face, cricking his neck back into the pillow.

Not wanting the pleasure to end, he removed her foothold. She crashed upon his rod, as he placed her toes in his mouth. The beauty's head spilled back between Bruce's legs, though she remained impaled with his spear.

The combined sensations were too much for her. Although she wasn't permitted to orgasm before the client, her secret was safe with Bruce. Exploding in an orgasmic fit, her brain tingled with stinging tremors. Her body shook, trying to douse the raging fire in her dark cavern.

Knight went so deep his bulbous head entered her colon. His manhood was squeezed so tight, it nearly snapped. Bruce lost control, blasting her flowing foxhole. Returning to an upright position, the curvaceous cutie dripped with DNA.

Joint grunts filled the air, harmonizing in a chorus of alto and soprano. She continued to ride him, saucing his cock in manly marinade. The two connected eyes, sharing one last jolt of lust. Leaning in, she kissed his lips. They infected each other with forbidden love.

Bruce broke the kiss, "Not tonight."

"What's wrong?" she asked, laying her head upon his chest. "You don't want to kiss me?"

"I...I just can't do this anymore."

A look of betrayal crossed her face. "Do *what* anymore? The visits? The sex? The *love*?"

"You know I can never turn that off."

"Then what can't you do? Was I wrong to think you were different than the others? Are you telling me I was crazy to have risked so much?"

"You're not crazy. I *am* different! Listen, your kiss is what keeps me alive. Yet, it's also the thing that kills me. It follows me home, haunting me...torturing me. It's all I think about. Then, I remember it'll never belong to me."

"My *heart* belongs to you. Isn't that enough?"

He looked down in guilt, running a hand through her red hair. "Of course it is. Though, every time I come back here...I wonder if you'll be gone. You could be moved...or killed. They'll never tell me."

She placed a hand on her stomach. "How about your *child*? Will *that* keep you coming back?"

"Child?" he asked in shock.

"I'm pregnant."

His face drained of all life. "Are you sure?"

"I'm sure it's *yours*, if that's what you're asking. I use birth control with everyone else. It was no mistake."

"Our child *won't* stay in this shithole! You won't either."

"It's a death sentence for us all," she warned.

"There's a forest at the edge of this place. Maybe there's a chance," Bruce said in hope.

"I heard...one girl escaped. She made it into Columbia...heading West. Some say it's only a legend. I've always believed it...I had to."

"The outer guards patrol this place. The odds aren't good," Bruce warned.

"Can it be any worse than staying here?" she asked, tearfully dismounting in a sea of sperm. Rising from the bed, she wiped herself clean. "When they find out I'm carrying a client's child...I'm dead anyway. If we can't be together, I don't want to live."

He rose, embracing the upset redhead. "We escape tonight."

She fearfully embraced him back. "No matter what happens...just know I love you."

"And I you." After putting on his pants, he looked her in the eyes. "You have my word. I'm not leaving this island without you *both*. Even If we leave in body bags...at least it's together."

She gasped, as fear gripped her heart. It was already late night, meaning the guard presence was at its lightest. No other clients or sex slaves were around. It was their best chance.

Bruce left the room alone, approaching a ski-masked, gun-toting guard at the exit door. The uniform was standard wear for the legendary Venezuelan whorehouse, *Paraíso*.

The man nodded, having seen Mr. Knight many times before. "How was the pussy tonight?" he asked in an accented voice. "Did the whore earn your money?"

Mr. Knight clinched his teeth, stopping at the door's edge. "You really wanna know how it felt?"

"Na, I already know," he bragged, insinuating he already nailed her.

Keeping his gaze forward, Bruce thrust an elbow into the guard's nose. Small splinters of bone pierced the man's smaller brain. A blank gaze peeked from the eye-slits, as his lifeless body crashed into the wall.

Mr. Knight's plan appeared to work, minus one major detail. As the masked guard fell back, his body triggered a wall alarm. "Now!" Bruce shouted.

The panicked redhead exited the room, joining his side. "Go on...I'll distract them. It's too late for me. I'm the one of value...run!"

"No!" he demanded. After kicking the door open, he lifted her into his arms. His feet immediately hit grainy dirt, causing him to slip. They both fell to the ground. Spotlights blazed the area, illuminating the distant forest.

"I can run," she said, kicking off her heels.

Although Bruce wanted to carry her, he followed her advice. Grabbing her hand, he pulled her along. She trailed behind him, already using every muscle she had, pushed to a speed never experienced.

"We're nearly there!" Mr. Knight yelled.

They reached the tree-line, as the curved redhead shouted, "We're really gonna make it!" Suddenly, a bullet pierced her back. The look of hope left her eyes, as she spilled into his arms. He caught her in his embrace, lowering her to the vegetation.

A few more bullets were fired, kicking up the dirt. Bruce didn't flinch, hoping to be shot. Cradling her in his arms, he said, "Stay alive...for our child!"

The life began to fade from her face. "I'm dying, Bruce."

"Listen...you must know. I've loved you since I first saw you. In that lineup...there was no one else there, but you and me."

"Thank you," she said.

"For what?"

"Freeing me." Her last words floated out, as her eyes slowly rolled.

Tears fell from the strong man. With them, his humanity was emptied. When she lost her life, Bruce also lost his. He'd never see her face again. At least, he didn't think so.

Bruce confusingly gazed at the redhead's lifeless face. It didn't make sense to him. The woman's name was Carolina, not Haley White. Though, the dying slave in his arms wore Ms. White's face.

In reality, Bruce was once Carolina's customer; Haley was his current prisoner. Carolina died years ago; Haley was still alive. He suddenly realized he was dreaming. *Wake up*, he told himself.

Returning to the present moment, a loud gasp filled Mr. Knight's lungs. He was in bed, mentally reliving a past nightmare. Far from Venezuela and *Paraíso,* he'd lived on Victor's secluded island for years. Though, the dream felt so real, his tightened fists swung at ghostly guards.

In his mind, he could still see ten men surrounding him with weapons. Eight of the guards wore ski masks. The two accompanying Victor did not. They were his personal security, Tommy Johns and Rico Rains.

Bruce could still see their rotten faces. He still felt Carolina's stiff body in his arms. Most of all, he remembered Victor Cruz's words. "Kill him. Let the two rot together."

"Do we bury them, sir?" a masked guard asked.

Victor paused. "Proper graves are for loyal slaves. Toss the traitors to the dogs."

"No!" Bruce shouted, charging the men. He took down six masked guards immediately.

Mr. Cruz watched in marvel. One guard lifted his gun, which Knight expertly kicked away. Then, the opponent was head-butted. The limp body was hurled into the eighth and final masked enemy. It broke his neck like a living arrow.

Bruce turned his sights upon Victor. "Deal with him!" Cruz yelled.

Rico Rains stepped up first. As he fired his weapon, Bruce dropped downward, anticipating the move. Sweeping Rico's knees, the guard fell upon his back. Bruce pummeled the man's face with tense fists. He'd repeat the act years later.

Before he could do fatal damage, Tommy Johns fired a shot into Bruce's shoulder. The injured Knight lunged once more, knocking the gun from Tommy's hand. Victor watched in amazement, as a spirited brawl continued.

Unfortunately for Bruce, his shoulder wound was an easy target. By irritating it, Tommy gained the advantage. Able to free his gun, he knocked Bruce out with a blow. Aiming his weapon, he prepared for a kill.

Victor interrupted. "I've changed my mind. This one can be of use."

Anger filled Tommy's face. "He'll take revenge."

"I'm counting on that. Though, by the time we're done with him...it won't be us he punishes."

"Who then?"

"Slaves," Victor said. "Take him to a holding cell."

Bruce returned to consciousness, dragged toward *Paraíso*. He watched a bloody Rico disrespectfully grab Carolina's body. "The dogs will love her!" he shouted, wiping the blood from his face.

Mr. Knight rose from his bed. Before forcing the painful memories from his mind, he was harshly reminded that he and Haley weren't *much* different. While she was kept for sex, he was kept to abduct and break her. Either way, they both served Victor's needs.

He wiped a handful of sweat. Although he'd be able to kill the memories, Haley's face would keep the feelings alive.

*****

Tired and shaken, Bruce silently led Haley to the breeder's doctor. She looked back at him, hoping he'd say something to her. "What will they do to me?"

"I don't know," he said coldly. After his nightmare, he was reminded of something. *Engaging in any emotions will get her killed. I can't risk that again. She's not my friend...not my lover...she's my prisoner.*

Haley could tell from the look in his eyes, he was in pain. Returning her gaze forward, she continued toward the exam room. Like Bruce, her thoughts turned to doubt. *Maybe I was wrong. Maybe all he felt was lust...nothing else. Maybe he's just a guard after all.*

Arriving in the exam room, she was greeted by Dr. Thomas Gray and a tanned nurse. The doctor's head was cleanly shaven, as his grayish eyes matched his name. "Recline on the table...feet in the stirrups," he ordered.

A nervous, nude Haley climbed onto a medical table. Bruce looked away, knowing unethical moments were common during examinations. Though in that world, ethics were always the exception, never the rule. As long as Dr. Gray didn't have vaginal sex with her, Mr. Knight wasn't authorized to stop it.

The curvy redhead reclined on the table, placing her ankles into cuffed stirrups. They were locked tight, assuring she'd stay still. After taking her blood pressure, the doctor took his seat in-between Haley's spread legs.

"Thermometer," he said to the nurse.

The obedient woman handed him the instrument. It was longer than the average thermometer. A digital head topped off a 12-inch stem. Activating it, he placed the probe at her slit.

"Lubricant doctor?" the nurse asked.

"She's already very wet," he said. Bruce looked up in shock. Haley's embarrassment was shown by a red face. She gasped, as Doctor Gray inserted the temperature probe into her moist crepe.

This isn't so bad, she thought to herself. Expecting it to stop at a shallow point, the progression continued. As it passed her g-spot, she stiffened. It kept sinking deeper, as her body tensed with each progressing inch.

"How deep do you need to go?" Haley asked.

"Quiet!" he scolded.

Haley obeyed, remembering slaves don't ask, they just do. She shut her eyes as the probe entered her tight cervical ring. Freaking out, Ms. White gripped onto the probe, trying to stop it from entering. "Nurse, deal with this!"

The nurse grabbed Haley's hands, pulling them back behind her head. A pair of cuffs was already there, chained to the wall. "I promise, I won't do it again," Haley begged.

"You're right," the nurse said, locking her wrists into place.

Continuing his job, the doctor ventured deeper into the depths of the womb. With each pressurized moment, Haley wiggled. Disappointment filled his face as the thermometer reached its end.

"Now, we wait," he said, watching the redhead's puffed lips constrict upon the probe. Since she didn't have control of her thigh muscles, it wasn't easy. Finally, a pulsating beep sounded. He quickly withdrew the long instrument, causing Haley's vagina to tighten more. Upon removal, he studied it. "98.6 degrees. Not ovulating." He turned towards Bruce. "You'll be charged with this task daily. Not a day will be missed, understand?"

"Tell me why?"

"The day her body temperature rises...roughly two degrees, ovulation begins. At that time...you'll inform Victor. She must be bred by day's end."

A worried look crossed Haley's face, matching Bruce's. "Fine," he answered.

The nurse bagged the thermometer, handing it to the guard. Dr. Gray announced his next step. "I'll need a sterile urine sample."

"Where's the bathroom?" Haley asked.

"Not necessary, slave. I'll bring the bathroom to you," he said, swabbing her meatus slit. Gasping, Haley looked toward Bruce again. He helplessly looked away. The nurse handed Dr. Gray a catheter tube, open at one end, bagged at the other. Spreading her tiny hole, he entered the lubed snake into her urethra.

Haley's inhalation sucked all air from the room. The tube's journey took a minute, keeping her in tense suspense.

"Relaxing will make this easier," the doctor assured her. She tried to obey, though couldn't fight the pressurized feeling in her urethra. Finally, the long catheter entered her bladder. Unknown to Haley, a stream of forced urine flowed, exiting into the specimen bag. "It stays until full," he said, moving on to his next task.

Standing up, he approached Haley's side. Fear filled her eyes, arousing the doctor. He moved to Haley's D-cup breasts. Groping the natural busts of beauty, he squeezed the mounds from their curvaceous base.

First he checked for lumps or abnormalities. His ungloved fists tightened, engorging her breasts to a bursting point. Each one was pulled outwards, extended and swelled in lust.

Her nipples nearly launched from their aureoles, pushed to their deep red limits. The doctor studied the thick, long shape. It was clear they'd be perfect for breastfeeding.

Moving his hands up the tear-shaped balloons, he continued to choke them of life. Finding no oddities, his hands arrived at her nipples. Dr. Gray rolled the missiles between his fingers.

Haley quietly moaned. As the tugging motion began, chills shot across her entire body. Every pore stood on end from the altering sensations. Dr. Gray watched closely, trying to spot any discharge from the milk ducts. They remained dry.

Seeing his patient's face tense, he continued the motion. As his actions increased, the combined sensations of warmth and cold increased. *Don't worry, you can't orgasm just from nipple play,* she assured herself. Within moments, she was proven wrong.

Without warning, Ms. White quivered in gentle orgasm. Lighter than a vaginal quake, it was like a magical stem connected her nipples and pleasure-box. A soft moan filled the air, as her trapped arms and legs shook with desire.

Jealousy filled Bruce. He knew she'd orgasm by the end of the exam, though didn't expect it so quickly. As the doctor returned to his seat, Mr. Knight grew even more uneasy.

Dr. Gray pushed the urine bag aside, freeing the pathway to her vagina. "Speculum," he announced to the nurse.

She handed a metal object in the shape of a duck's beak. He smeared a glob of cold lube inside her vaginal lips. The nurse assisted in parting the red sea, as Dr. Gray entered the speculum inside her.

As it was entered, he adjusted the position. Pressing a lever, the beak slowly opened, stretching her vaginal canal wide. Haley tensed, as the doctor continued beyond his usual width. He kept going, until she was dilated three-inches.

"A work of art," he proclaimed, staring down in an abyss of pink perfection. Her cervix was tight and free of disease. The only secretions present were of lust. He leaned in to sniff her scent, as his eyes rolled from the flowery fragrance.

Grabbing an air spatula, he aimed it into the stretched hole. "I will perform a pap smear," he said, scraping cell samples from her vaginal walls. Afterward, he handed it to the nurse, who sprayed and carefully stored it for testing. A contaminated misreading would not be tolerated.

He lubed two fingers. Bruce was on edge, ready to react. However, he had no business doing so. "Now for the bimanual examination and vaginal fluid test.

Haley cringed, looking over at Bruce. From the pale look on his face, she knew it wasn't something good. Using the speculum stretched hole, he forced the fingers into her tender tunnel.

She gasped, feeling the long appendages slide deeper. Using his free hand, he pressed down on her outer-pubic area. Her breath increased, as her g-spot was squeezed both internally and externally.

After minutes of outer-massage, he redirected his free hand, keeping the internal fingers inside. Two unoccupied fingers headed toward Haley's sensitive rectum. Already drenched with a mixture of natural juices and lube, he worked the digits into her tight sphincter. Pulling at her restraints again, Ms. White tensed at anal invasion.

Checking her fertility was his job, forcing an orgasm was his pleasure. After spinning all-fingers in circular motions, her sensitive nerves were stimulated. Confirming her inner walls were healthy, he began the fluid test.

Using a forceful probing of her holes, he landed hard thrusts into her swelling g-spot. The intensity made Haley tremble, unsure whether to cry or cum. It wouldn't surprise her if both emotions kicked in.

Dr. Gray's eyes widened like a wolf seeing red. His motions sped up. In a lustful frenzy, he alternated, pumping each hole separately. Haley began to moan, catching Bruce's attention like winter flu.

He studied her tensed eyelids, shaking along with her lip. She tried to fight a massive orgasm, though was losing the battle. Her vaginal tunnel heated up, as the dual sensations plunged away.

As Haley's body naturally pushed, her catheter flowed like the yellow river. The specimen bag swelled with sample. All thoughts of vanity vanished, as her shame only added to her increasing arousal.

Saving his best trick for last, Dr. Gray thrust all fingers at once. Forced to her sexual edge, the curvy patient cried out. "Push!" the doctor ordered. "Push hard, let go!" Arching her back, she obeyed his command. Every muscle tensed, pushing downward.

Suddenly, a blast of clear fluid rushed out. His ungloved hands were shot from her cannon, as a squirting of g-spot fluid drenched him. "Oh my!" Haley shouted, shuddering like a wet poodle in winter. Even with her arms and legs trapped, her vaginal lips still managed to quiver. They longed to milk every drop.

Dropping to his knees, Dr. Gray shut the speculum, tossing it away. Using his tongue, he forced himself deep inside her creamy cavern. Spinning in a tornado, he lapped every sweet drop from her.

Bruce tensed in jealousy, seeing the doctor lower his scrubs. Placing a hand on his weapon, he stepped forward. He almost hoped Dr. Gray would attempt vaginal penetration. It would give him an excuse to blast the man with bullets. "Don't even think about it," Mr. Knight warned.

Heeding Bruce's advice, the doctor opted to jerk himself. The more he sucked her nectar, the harder he got. A sugary sweetness coated his senses, pumped through his blood. It acted as a form of human Viagra. His average-sized cock swelled with pleasure, as he yanked hard and fast. Within moments, he squirted a large load on the exam room floor.

"That's enough," Bruce insisted, seeing Haley's face sour.

"He's biting me!" she cried out.

The doctor became addicted, unable to break away. Mr. Knight walked over, unclenching Dr. Gray's jaw. Yanking him off, he flung the spasming man to the floor. "That's your last warning!"

Wiping his mouth, the doctor tried to hide his embarrassment. There was no longer any doubt why Haley was chosen. She was so pure, ensuring that her heir would be perfect in every way. In Victor's eyes, *that* meant being a boy.

"She is approved to deliver the heir. Dare I say, she defines what a breeder should be. The moment she ovulates, you'll inform Mr. Cruz. In the meantime, you must keep a close eye on this breeder. Protect her from others. As hard as she is to resist...I'd even watch yourself."

CHAPTER SIX

Haley White entered a beautiful breeding suite, featuring a four-poster bed draped with silk curtains. A plush mattress was covered in satin sheets and blankets, crowded with overstuffed pillows. Marble tiles decorated the floors, matching the elegance of the crown-molded walls.

A basket of freshly peeled oranges adorned her room. Next to that was a pitcher of citrus punch, made with island fruits. She ran for the food, taking a big juicy bite. Her eyes nearly rolled backward, savoring each swallow. "I'm starving."

It was a far cry from the slave quarters. Clearly, her life was being upgraded, as her worth equaled a rare gem. In Victor's mind, better conditions encouraged male conception. He obviously knew nothing about the process.

Haley gazed around the room in awe. "Wow. I never even had this back home."

Bruce looked downward, realizing she was falling into Victor's trap. He shuddered to think about a fate of possible failure. "Only the best for the breeders."

"There are others?"

He hesitated. "There *were*."

"*Were*? Where are they now?" she asked in a worried manner. Her gulp was coordinated with another bite of the orange.

"That's not for me to disclose."

"Sorry," she said, eating again. "I don't want to get you in trouble."

"It's not your job to worry about me," Bruce instructed, keeping his tone emotionless. "*I* watch over *you*."

The hungry girl paused, staring in his eyes. For a moment, she started to believe in him again. *He watches over me...cares for me.* Then, she focused on one of his words. "Just doing your *job*," she said.

"Right. You shouldn't overeat; a full course meal is coming. The rush of food will make you sick...having eaten so little over the month."

"Just a few more bites." She gnawed it down. "I'm sorry...I should offer you one."

"They're for you. Besides, I get all the fruit I want."

She paused, finishing off the orange. "Must be nice getting everything you want."

"I never said *everything*. You *do* realize...there's more to life than oranges?"

"Oh, I didn't mean to imply anything. I just forget that everyone isn't a slave, like me."

"Never assume anything...especially around here. Besides, you're not a slave...not anymore. You're a breeder."

"Can I leave?"

"No."

"Then I'm a slave."

"Give Mr. Cruz what he wants...and you'll never want again. You'll have no reason to return home. Not even your family."

"Who says I had one?" she asked.

"Surely there's someone waiting for you? Worried about you?"

Sadness painted her eyes. "I have no family...and *that* includes *Victor Cruz*. What about you? Who's been waiting for Mr. Knight? A wife, kids, parents? Why do you stay?"

He looked down in pain. "Everyone dear to me...died long ago. I have no reason to leave."

"But what if you did? What if...you find someone worth leaving for?"

"I told you...they died long ago. There's no one left for me."

"Well, I guess we're not *that* different, after all."

"No more questions. I've put you in enough danger. The less we know about each other, the safer you'll be."

"Right," she said, turning away in hurt. "Oh, one more thing. May I ask...where you'll sleep?"

"Outside your door...guarding it."

"So, you'll sleep standing up? I don't get it."

"Not quite standing...more like leaning. And it's more of a twilight coma. It's an old military trick."

"Military? American?"

"Listen, this has to stop. You're supposed to be...broken...void of spirit. Questions prove thought. Thoughts prove individuality. Around here, individuals die. Don't you realize it's my job to report to Mr. Cruz? One word of this...you'd be killed."

"But you won't say a thing."

"And why not?"

"Because...like I said. We're not *that* different. In fact...we're very much the same."

He shut his eyes, realizing the complicated mess he had made. A door knock interrupted the awkward moment. Bruce grabbed his gun, creeping towards it. "Who is it?"

"The meal bearers."

He opened the door, as a cart rolled in. A silver platter was uncovered. It was Caribbean pork, glazed with sugar and sautéed onions. Rice and beans were on the side. The servants exited, as Haley's mouth watered. "I don't know what that is...but if it tastes like it smells...I'm in for a treat."

"As I said...only the best for the breeders." He turned to exit the room.

"Wait. Are you sure you can't join me for dinner? I mean, who's watching?"

Bruce looked around the room, seeing many opportune camera spots. "Maybe no one. Maybe everyone. Maybe Victor. If I can give you one piece of advice, it's this. The moment you feel safe in this place...will be your last."

He exited, shutting the door behind him. Haley sighed, sitting down to a lonely meal. Although thankful for the improved settings, she knew it could end at any moment.

*****

The hallway was dark. Bruce stood guard, appearing to be awake. His eyes were half-open, body slanted against Haley's door. In reality, he was asleep, yet still maintaining a mental presence. Such skill was rare, though it was one of the gifts his Army training gave him.

Another gift was an ability to travel the world. When his time expired, he headed to South America, seeking out a different culture. After he discovered *Paraíso,* his life would never be the same.

Those days were long gone. He hadn't been a soldier in decades, nor a brothel customer. However, terrors flashed inside his mind like it was just yesterday. In his mind, he was masked and bound, forced off a plane. The humid island air baked his skin, as he was shuttled to a warehouse.

Hung from chains, his naked body dangled, feet hovered off the ground. Sweat poured from him, as the hot sun cooked the concrete block building. Given little food or water, he was denied the fuel of fight. Twice a day, he was tortured in one form or another.

Daily, he was whipped with cattails. Tommy and Rico took turns beating him in revenge for their downed brethren. One at a time, they whipped his muscular back, butt, and legs.

Much like Haley, he was beaten into submission. However, he took much longer to break. Even after two months of whippings, Bruce remained stubborn. He was occasionally given slack, so his arms and legs wouldn't atrophy or gangrene.

After each session, female slaves were brought in to soothe his wounds. Towards the end of the month, he looked void of life. He was ready to die, until Victor arrived.

Appearing from the shadows, the master offered a devilish deal. Two sex slaves were with him, along with Tommy and Rico. "You are a strong man, Mr. Knight," Victor said. "You are also stubborn. One trait I admire, the other I do not."

"Kill me already, damn you!" Bruce demanded.

"If death claims you, it will not come from my hand."

"Why the hell not?"

"Because I see something in you...your true nature. Mr. Knight, you are like us."

"Never! I don't kill innocents!"

"The sex slave? I owned her...you tried to steal her. She was a top earner...I gained nothing in taking her life. So, in effect, Mr. Knight...*you* killed her."

"Fuck you!" he screamed.

"Serve me...and your life can be of worth for once."

"I'll never break!"

"I believe that. Though, just in case, *girls*..." Victor ordered, pointing at the prisoner.

The two buxom brunettes approached the chained man. As they touched him, he tried to pull away. They held him still. One began stroking his cock gently, as the other knelt down, massaging his testicles.

"Get off me!" he shouted. Though, as hard as he tried to fight it, his massive cock began to grow thick and wide. "Why the hell are you doing this?"

"Because, Mr. Knight. I've shown you hell...now, I offer a glimpse into paradise."

The stroking slave joined the other upon her knees. Aiming his bulbous offering at her face, she stretched her mouth open, wetting his spear. The second slave rose between his legs, engulfing his balls fully.

He gasped, overtaken by pleasure. The cock-sucking slave swallowed the spear to the base, as the other sucked the sack into her throat. Their joint rhythm was timed to perfection, since it was a specialty at the Venezuelan brothel.

While sucking his balls, a line of saliva spilled from the slave's lips. She collected it on a finger, and then parted Bruce's ass cheeks. He wiggled, though couldn't stop it from being forced into his sphincter.

Both mouths continued to suck away, as the anal finger poked his virgin prostate. The hanging man swayed from side to side, tightening every muscle. The more he tensed, the harder he got. His face cringed, trying to stop an ounce of pleasure from showing.

Victor approached him closely, stroking Bruce's face. "Don't fight the pleasure, embrace it. This can be yours...everyday...every night. Swear loyalty to me, and you're forgiven."

"Never!" he shouted, as the sucking increased. Regaining strength, he struggled to pull from their hold.

"Then let me remind you of your other option. Gentlemen," he said, nodding at Tommy and Rico. The two men approached Bruce with whips in hand. They began lashing his upper back.

The stinging pulses made each muscle tense more. His cheeks tightened upon the probing finger, forcing a flood of prostate fluid from his slit. It made his cock engorge, growing thicker and longer with desire. Streams of saliva seeped down his rod, into his crack.

Chills covered his skin with each new crackling of the whip. As strong as he was, there was no defying human nature. Bruce was still just a man.

Grunting outward, he broke down. Unleashing his fury, a river of cum rushed from him. His ass cheeks tensed, fire flowed from his hose. The second slave disconnected from his testes, joining her partner at his bulbous head. Her finger stayed, milking every last drop.

Removing her mouth, the first slave continued jerking. A shotgun of cum sprayed their faces. It was heavy and thick, having been dormant for a while. Streams of semen saturated their skin and hair, each sharing the soaking. The two fought for their share, swallowing every drop like edible gold.

Tommy and Rico's laughs filled the humid room, as their whipping continued. "Disengage girls," Victor ordered. They immediately backed away. "Each day will begin and end with your two choices. Your life can be either one. You decide," he said, exiting with the slaves.

"Do we stop?" Tommy asked.

Victor paused. "Did I tell you to stop?"

They continued whipping the spent prisoner.

Bruce managed to hold out another two weeks, eventually breaking. Victor returned with Tommy and Rico.

"Will I have to kill slaves?" Mr. Knight asked.

"Perhaps," Victor answered nonchalantly. Before Bruce could decline, Mr. Cruz continued. "Only when they deserve it. However, I ask you not to waste thought on lives taken, but lives you'll save."

"Save?"

"For every slave you break, they'll never try to escape. For every heart you empty of emotion, they'll never fall in love. Save them from the fate of your *precious* Carolina. Don't you see? Your love killed her. She was fine, until you gave her hope. You can't save her anymore...though, there are many others you can save."

As much as Bruce wanted to die, he finally found a reason to give in. *Those innocent girls are no different than Carolina. I can't let them die like her.* "I'll do it!" he yelled, stopping Victor at the door.

A wicked smiled crossed Mr. Cruz's face, turning towards Tommy and Rico. "Go ahead, gentlemen."

"I said I'd do it!" Bruce shouted.

"The first answer is what I want to hear. The second...is what you really mean. I'll give it another week, just to make sure."

The whipping began again, more brutal than before. Knowing it was their last chance at revenge, Tommy and Rico punished Bruce. Shaking with pain, Bruce warned, "You better kill me now.

Someday...I'll be the one with the whip." Hearing the challenge, both men hurled a lash at the back of his head.

Bruce woke from his nightmare, thrust back to current reality. In the hallway, he was confronted by Tommy Johns. A hungry look filled his eyes. Bruce stepped up to him. "This area is off limits to your patrol."

"Just checking on the breeder...making sure she's...*comfortable*," Tommy said with a grin.

"That's not your concern. I don't want to see you in here again...understand?"

"Perfectly," he said. Turning to exit, his laughter filled the hallway.

*****

Bruce entered the room, finding an empty bed. His heart jumped, as the first thought entered his mind, *They got to her*. However, he knew that wasn't a possibility, since he would've snapped into action.

She couldn't have escaped, he told himself. Suddenly, his thoughts were interrupted by flowing water. *The shower!* He chastised himself. Quietly peeking into the bathroom, he was struck by a blinding sight.

Natural sunbeams shone from an overhead skylight, highlighting milky skin. Clear shower-glass revealed Haley's curvaceous body. Flowing water cascaded off her breasts like a multi-tier waterfall, tapped from the purest point of earth. Her fire-red hair changed tones, darkening with wetness.

As she lathered her skin with soap, she shined with angelic radiance. A direct sunbeam struck her, giving her a glistening set of wings. Bruce thought back to the night he picked Carolina from the lineup. She was wearing body sparkles, which glistened in the neon lighting.

A gasp suddenly filled the room, as Haley noticed him watching. He looked away, saying, "Sorry. I...came to tell you...it's time to take your body temperature."

"OK," she said, taking one last rinse through the water.

Stepping out of the shower, he handed her a towel, continuing to look away. She patted herself dry, dropping it on the floor. "It's nothing you haven't seen before."

He nodded. "You were a slave before. Now you're Victor's property."

"Am I really?"

"You still doubt that?"

"The day I broke...I submitted to you...and you alone. No one else."

"We all belong to him...in one way or another. Tell me, where would you like to do it?"

"Do it?"

He held up the temperature gauge. "See if you're ovulating?"

"The bed's fine, I guess."

She led the way, lying flat on the soft mattress. Spreading her legs wide, beads of water clung to her thighs. The smell of cocoa butter teased his senses, causing him to fight his urge of ravaging her.

"The doctor said, it's more effective if you get on your hands and knees," he instructed.

"Whatever you say...master," she teased, turning over.

"I told you...that title belongs to Mr. Cruz."

Getting into a doggy-style position, she turned her head towards him. A playful smirk accompanied a fire in her eyes. It burned brighter than before her breaking. "A title is made of only words. Nothing more."

He was shocked, as she looked forward again. Kneeling down, he ran a tongue up her soft fold. She gasped in surprise. Spreading her hind lips, Bruce eased the long temperature gauge through her pink canal. Haley tensed, feeling it slide deeper, entering her cervix and womb.

"Just relax," he assured her. "You'll get used to this."

"For how long?"

"For as long as you produce males."

"You mean...I'll just keep having babies?"

"You're a breeder...that's your purpose in life now." A digital beeping sounded from the probe. Withdrawing it, he examined the numbers. "Normal...you're not ovulating."

Lying back down, she said, "How many chances will I get...to have a boy?"

He hesitated, deciding to tell her. "One."

"Just tell me...will I be killed?"

Bruce looked downward. "Most likely."

"Have any others survived?"

"One."

"Why her?"

"She was the first...Victor loved her."

"Where is she?"

"Since you're clearly not going to stop asking dangerous questions...I'll make you a deal."

"Anything."

"I'll show you...if you promise to stop."

"Deal," she said with a wink.

*****

Bruce led Haley to the compound's slave wing. Exiting into the daylight, twenty-foot walls encapsulated an array of buildings. Any exterior sight or chance of escape was impossible. Since Bruce made the guard schedule, he knew where trouble was and where it wasn't.

Walking the outdoor hallway, Haley inhaled the salty air. The sound of distant waves teased her ears, as her eyes perked up. "The beach?"

"The sea. A beach is where you vacation. In case you haven't noticed, this is no vacation."

"I've noticed. I've just never seen it before."

"I abducted you from Florida...how's that possible?"

"I was in the central part. Besides, in a state run institution...there are no field trips. After that...I bounced around a few foster families...not long enough for outings. The last guy...he wasn't the beach type!"

"You were an orphan?"

"Born and raised. Don't know much about my real family. I can remember as a kid, wishing they'd just reappear one day. I was so angry, lost. The truth is...I don't have anyone. Never did...never will."

Bruce exhaled, knowing the feeling of emptiness. "Well, maybe...before you claim Victor's side, I can at least make one wish come true."

"An instant family?"

"No. The sea. We're on an island. I can do that much."

She smiled at his kindness.

He stopped walking, momentarily lost in her beauty.

"What?" she asked.

"You just reminded me of someone."

"Who?"

"Someone I loved...someone I lost," he said, moving on. Seeing it was a sensitive subject, Haley didn't inquire.

*****

Upon entering the building, a mixture of moans and cries filled their ears. "You say nothing...do nothing in here. In fact, do yourself a favor...look straight, keep walking. Do you understand?" Bruce warned her.

She nodded, though her curiosity was peaked. Ignoring Bruce's advice, she turned her head towards the noise. They entered a massive room, stocked with hundreds of mattresses. An endless collection of slaves was in the process of getting brutally fucked.

The male participants were customers, not guards. There were a few blond, fair-skinned Anglos. Most were of Hispanic or Eastern European descent. Ms. White gazed at a blond being banged anally. Her hair was yanked back so hard, the girl's neck nearly snapped. A brunette slave rode a black man cowgirl style, while another rode his face in reverse position.

There was a Spanish woman receiving double anal, and double vaginal sex. Two cocks were forced inside both holes. She screamed from the pressure, finally passing out in silence.

These must be new recruits...a much larger group, Haley guessed. Her thoughts changed when she recognized one of the slaves. The particular brunette was in a missionary position, slapped profusely in the face. An obese man pumped his small cock into her, getting off on the bloody canvas he created.

Although it took Haley a moment to recognize the slave, it was a girl from her original group. Carried off the stage, she had been proclaimed *rotten* by Victor, removed for her vaginal scent.

Tears filled Haley's eyes, looking back at Bruce. He shuddered with sickness, clearly affected by the room. The look on his face was more than concern...it was personal. His pain came from a deeper source than just observance. Of course, he'd never tell her what he did in there.

Looking back at the mattresses, two more faces were familiar to her. They had disappeared after failing the blowjob test. They were both being choked, while three men filled every one of their holes. Their faces were blue from being denied much needed oxygen.

One of the girls shifted her gaze, making contact with Haley. Although she wasn't able to speak, her eyes screamed, *help!* It suddenly became clear they weren't new recruits. They were *throwaways*. Not good enough for premium service, they were essentially a clearance rack. Customers were brought to the island, offered free reign for a wholesale price.

The multitude of sights rushed the redhead. Panic filled her, trembling with flashbacks of her own training. Even worse, she imagined what her life could've been. She froze, shutting her eyes in fright. Suddenly, a hand grasped hers. "It's OK...this isn't your life anymore," Bruce assured her.

"You have to stop this from happening!"

"Maybe someday," he said in defeated hopelessness. "Let's get out of here."

*****

He guided her into a media room. There, a TV monitor was recording a scene. A thick pane of glass filled a wall. Behind the glass was a beautiful room, equipped with a double mirror. A sexy woman was in process of seducing an unattractive, yet powerful man.

Wiping tears from her eyes, Haley refocused her attention on the scene. Bruce pointed at the blond woman. *"That's* what happened."

"What?"

"You asked what happened to the first failed breeder. The others were killed in frustration."

"The baby girls as well?"

"No," he said in a disturbed manner. "Though, they'd have been better off."

"Where are they?"

"Scattered across the world. Sold to the worst kind of scum."

"But...they can't even be that old," she said, stopping with a gasp. "I can't have a girl. I won't let them take her!"

"Don't torture yourself with possibilities...it'll only make it worse."

"And this woman? Why did she live over the others? What's so special about her?"

"Mr. Cruz always said...she could make him spill his deepest, darkest secrets with one gaze. That kind of power has worth."

"What's that have to do with sex slavery?"

"Oh, this woman's no sex slave. She's a spy."

"Spy?"

"You see the man she's with?"

Haley studied the tan skinned man, who the curvy blond passionately rode. "I do."

"That's a president."

"Of what country?"

"It doesn't matter...she's done them all. Prime Ministers, Kings, even clergy."

"That still doesn't explain the spying part?"

"I'll let her explain," he said, turning up the recording's volume. Joint puffs of air filled the mic as the woman leaned inward. "Tell me...your most inner secrets. Things your wife wouldn't even know."

Lust filled the man's face. He was hypnotized by her bouncing breasts and trusting blue eyes. "We developed a new kind of bomb...can wipe away a small country. The project was named...after you."

"Thank you, baby. Is it nuclear?" she asked.

"No...something of a top secret nature."

"Tell me more!" she demanded, picking up speed and intensity. The harder she rode him, the more information he spilled.

Bruce lowered the sound. "There's your answer."

"What good is *that* information to you?"

"To me...it's useless. Victor on the other hand...can use it in a number of ways. He can blackmail the man for money. Or...he can blackmail his country for weapons."

"No!"

"His power is unchecked."

"Will I...become that? I'm not sure death would be worse."

He looked Haley in the eyes. "Produce a male...and you won't have to worry about either one."

CHAPTER SEVEN

The temperature probe beeped loudly. A heavy tone echoed off the walls, as Bruce removed it. He examined the numbers, while cringing his face. "100.3," he announced in disappointment.

Haley gasped, giving him a nervous look. "Ovulating?"

"It appears so." His voice was grim.

"What happens next? What happens after the baby? Will I get to see you again?"

"Take one day at a time."

"Will I?"

He looked down. "After the birth, no. There's a long time between now and then."

"So what happens now?"

"I'll inform Victor. You go to preparation."

Panic suddenly overcame Haley, as she began to cry. "I don't want a baby."

"Don't do this to yourself," Bruce said. "It'll only make things harder."

Ms. White wiped her tears away, forcing herself to face reality. "What's preparation? Will it hurt?"

"No. I hear they bathe you. Never witnessed it with my own eyes...though I believe they doll you up for Mr. Cruz. The conception will take place tonight...8 P.M.," he said in disgust.

"There must be a way to stop this," she begged.

"Only death could stop Victor from getting his heir. As long as I'm by your side...that won't be an option. Let's go."

Haley exhaled, standing up. She stopped one last time. "Tell me something."

"Ask."

"Did you protect the other breeders...the way you protect me?"

He paused, knowing it would make things easier to just say, *yes.* However, he couldn't do it. "No."

Rare satisfaction crossed her face. She'd never really felt like anyone cared, until *that* moment. She suddenly had something to hang on to. It was a long shot, though she believed Bruce Knight would save her from Victor's breeding. "I'm ready."

*****

Haley arrived in the preparation area. It was a Roman-style bath with a circular tub. The jetted water was warmed to comfort, along with the room's natural temperature. Three beautiful women in white greeted her. Each one donned the grace of an ancient goddess, in-fitting with the theme.

One pale blond glowed like gold, with eyes of light blue. Two tanned brunettes joined her. Their hair was darker than the blackest cat, eyes to match. "Come," the blond said in a Scandinavian accent.

The nervous redhead approached in a robe. The two brunettes held her hands, gently leading her forward. They felt Ms. White's hand tremble, as she followed their direction.

Arriving at the tub's edge, the blond blocked the breeder's path. Angelic hands parted the robe, unveiling a set of curves equal to her own. Sliding the terrycloth to the floor, the woman devoured Haley with her eyes. Then she quickly returned to her job.

The blond goddess dropped her short, white dress to the floor. She stepped backwards into the tub. Descending one step, her finger wagged for the redhead to follow. Dipping a feminine foot into the warm suds, Haley was re-guided by the careful hands of the brunettes. Taking another step down, the breeder was up to her waist in swirling water.

Her hands were released, as the brunettes also undressed. Entering the pool, each took a spot at Haley's opposite sides. The women formed a triangle of sexuality. The mysterious girls reached for three pink sponges.

Victor had the local coral reefs torn apart, combing the ocean floor. His goal was to ensure the softest, highest quality sea wool on earth. As his breeder would soon discover, he found exactly what he desired.

Dousing the wet sponges with imported body soap, the women began their cleansing ritual. The two brunettes placed the soft scrubbers upon Haley's separate breasts.

They squeezed, letting the sudsy water cascade her curves. The heat stung Haley's nipples, engorging them into weapons. Her red daggers pierced the moldable material. As the sponge was pressed inward the nubs slowly inverted into the aureoles.

A natural citrus scent filled Ms. White's nose. She shut her eyes, as the sponges danced in a romantic spin. After a few moments of teasing, one brunette moved upward, while the other downward. Trails of bubbles were left in their wake. The upper sponge bathed the upper teardrop, while the lower serviced the bottom.

One sponge continued across the diaphragm, up the sensitive part of the throat. The bottom sponge veered downward, soaking Haley's pale stomach. The curves of her hips were traced, covered in bubbles. Her cavernous belly was rimmed, as an ocean of suds flowed inside.

Each new touch tingled Haley's body in a different way. None of them compared to the blond's offering. The glowing goddess dipped her sponge beneath the water's edge. Rising between Haley's legs, it crawled along the submerged lips, washing the trimmed red pubic hair. Her natural color contrasted the water like fire in glass.

A gasp sounded from the redhead's throat as the pliable sponge was worked inside her puffed lips. Squeezed tightly, it was reshaped, fit snugly into her cavern. Molded to replicate her unique canal, the soapy invader was unleashed. As the sponge expanded, it filled her hole. The breeder's breath increased, feeling it cleanse her birthing lair.

The sponge was thrust deeper, making Haley's legs tremble. After its removal, the clit was scrubbed, inciting a soft moan. Extra time was spent there, rubbed in a circular pattern.

One brunette goddess returned to wash Haley's breasts, alternating between strokes. The other slowly washed the backside, dragging a trail down the backbone's ridge. Arriving at her curved ass cheeks, she let the sponge slip inside. Rubbing in a wiping motion, she tickled the sensitive zone.

Completely stimulated and clean, the women placed a hand on Haley's shoulders. She was slowly lowered, dunked into the watery abyss by the bathing beauties. Giving herself to them, she was in their control. Her stomach disappeared, then her breasts, finally her head vanished.

Underneath the water, Haley forced her eyes open. The room light shone from above, highlighting the goddesses. Their hair flowed in angelic patterns, emulating her own. Six hands massaged her skin, ridding all soapy residue. Her lips were parted, along with her anus.

Two tubes were eased into both holes. A shocked Haley shuddered, trying to escape. She was held down. The water around her stopped swirling, beginning to rush through her body.

A rubber bulb was fit over the tub's jets, redirecting the flow into Haley's orifices. Not only was she cleaned externally, but internally as well. Her struggle continued, feeling the tubed water rush through her dual canals. By the time she filled, Ms. White felt like she'd burst. The rushing water mercifully stopped.

Nearing a drowning, Ms. White was pulled back up. Her face tensed, as the sensitive body stroking continued. A loud hum filled the air, as the jets were switched into a reverse-sucking pattern.

She humiliatingly expelled the enema back through the tubes. Her body cramped, as the goddess's massaged her breasts, stomach, and hair. Once fully emptied, the tubes were removed. The three nude women lifted her in their arms, carrying her from the tub. Her wet body was slid upon slick, heated tiles.

The nude goddesses dried her with Egyptian cotton towels. Filling their hands with premium lotion, they drowned every pore. The blond rubbed it upon Haley's feet, sliding up soft legs. She continued on, buttering glossy thighs, chafing the edge of vaginal lips.

Two sets of hands molested her breasts, caressing each inch with edible lotion. After every inch of skin was covered, they returned to her nipples. This time they squeezed the aureoles, setting the nerve endings aflame. Her appetizing nubs were extended with a light pulling motion, causing a pleasurable sting.

The blond continued to massage Haley's outer lips, moving into forbidden territory. Already soaked with desire, the lubed fingers wiggled their way into the strawberry crepe.

Ms. White squirmed, held down by her breasts. Two fingers slid into the watery slide like morning dew on grass. Slow, deep and deliberate strokes followed, making Haley tense up.

The blond reached her knuckles, as she added two fingers to the clit. While the breeder's love-button was pleasurably pinched, both brunettes sucked upon sweet nipples. Their tongues danced, raising every pore upon the tasty treats.

Overcome with lust, Haley moaned loudly. Both brunettes covered Haley's mouth, stopping her from alerting their forbidden act. Though, no one expected them to avoid such a tantalizing temptation.

The blond's finger-thrusts increased with speed, whipping the clit with blazing smacks and slaps. As much as the redheaded breeder wanted to fight it, the goddesses couldn't be denied.

Haley's muffled moans trickled out, as she shook in uncontrolled orgasm. Her body writhed across the wet floor, leaving a trail of lotion in her wake. Once the pleasure subsided, the blond withdrew her fingers. She sucked every drop of the sweet sap.

Rising, the women reached for separate buckets, scooping handfuls of mystery. Approaching Ms. White, they drizzled a sprinkling of body crystals upon her. Floating like sparkling snowflakes, Haley was covered from head to toe. She shut her eyes, letting each piece stick to her greased body.

From there, her hair was styled in a Roman goddess way, just like her handlers. The once-odd symbolism suddenly made sense to Haley. *Victor thinks he's a god. Therefore, the woman who bears his child must resemble a goddess.*

*****

Bruce exited Victor's office with his head hung low. Before he arrived there, he called a special meeting of the guards. Each one was lined up in submission before him. Tommy Johns and Rico Rains were present.

"Today there will be a schedule change. No one...and I mean, *no one*, is to guard the North side until 8:00. Victor ordered it himself."

"Why?" Tommy shouted.

"Did I give you permission to question my authority?"

"No," he defiantly said.

"That's no *sir*, to you!"

Tommy remained quiet, making sure to stare his boss down.

"All that's important...is you obey Mr. Cruz's orders. Do you understand?" Bruce asked the group.

"Yes, sir," they said in unison.

"Do you!" Bruce shouted in Tommy's face.

"I understand *exactly*...boss," he said in mockery.

After the meeting, Bruce entered Victor's office. The powerful man was on the phone, barking his usual orders. One look at Mr. Knight's serious face, made him hang up without warning. "What's wrong?" he asked.

"Nothing's wrong. In fact, I have good news."

"She's ovulating?"

"She is," Bruce said in a dispirited tone.

"With the look on your face...I'd think death's coming for you."

"Death comes for us all...it's just a matter of *when*," he cryptically said.

Victor squinted at the odd statement. "Some of us...sooner than later," he warned.

Bruce nodded in agreement. "She's being prepped as we speak. Tonight, I'll deliver her to your room," he said, attempting to exit.

"Not so fast, Mr. Knight."

"Something else, sir?"

"The time has finally come...a male heir! In these last hours, you will guard her as if your life depends on it. I don't need to remind you of that fact."

"I'll protect her...from the ones who can hurt her the most. You have my word."

"That's why you're my number one man. Now, go do your job."

After exiting, Bruce forced all emotion from his heart, punishing himself. *Damn you. Face the facts already. You're in too deep again! Let go of her!*

At that moment, he believed he was detached from Haley White. He entered her room ready to serve Victor's needs only. However, one gaze upon the sparkling beauty, and Mr. Cruz's needs, mattered not. From that moment, his only concern was the woman he loved. He finally admitted *that* she was in front of him.

Sprawled upon the bed, she wore a silk nightgown, no bra, panties, or shoes. The crystals reflected each tone of her red hair, making it shine in the neutral light.

Her pale skin glistened like the midday sun, making him squint strained eyes. Haley's full lips were traced in cherry red, matching her painted toes and fingernails. For the first time in his life, he saw beauty greater than Carolina. It was the first time she was second in his heart.

He tried to speak, though couldn't form the words. "I...I..." he gave up, continuing to gaze.

"How long do I have?" Haley asked.

"About two hours," he forced from his throat.

She sighed. "Is it wrong that I'm nervous?"

"Not at all."

"It's hard to believe. After tonight...my life will never be the same. Whatever happens."

"You're right about that," he blurted out. Walking over, he lifted her in his strong arms. She gasped, surprised at the unexpected act. She felt so secure, she didn't ask where he was taking her. It was a security she'd never experienced before.

Bruce headed towards the door, carrying the bejeweled beauty to a mystery. Wherever it was, she knew her best interest was at heart.

CHAPTER EIGHT

Massive concrete walls lined the compound's outer-rim. Four guard towers decorated each corner of the slave island. Occupying most of the landmass, only a stretch of white sand surrounded it.

After that, an endless ocean flowed to a lonely horizon-line. It appeared the world ended at that point, which wasn't lost on Mr. Cruz. If one of the slaves escaped, their only choice was a death by drowning.

Having received orders, all guards vacated the North side. That included the snipers in the towers. However, one man dared to defy the boss's orders. His name was Tommy Johns.

Peeking through the gun's magnified crosshairs, Mr. Johns searched for a golden nugget. He knew betrayal was Victor's least tolerated crime. One disloyal act could change Bruce's world. More importantly, it could also restore Tommy to a position he once occupied.

*****

Bruce carefully walked the halls of an emergency exit, safe from the eyes of trouble. Besides Victor and Tommy, only *he* knew of its existence. The sound of rushing waters filled Haley's ears, as a smile crossed her face. She didn't even have to see the source, as the two exited into the waning light. A low setting sun set the horizon ablaze, burning pastel reds, yellows, pinks, and oranges.

Ms. White's eyes opened wide, as excitement painted her face like a child at Christmas. "A wish come true," she said.

He set her down on the bleached sands. The water still owned its aqua tone, lit by the last rays of daylight. "Is it everything you hoped?"

"More than I ever imagined. Inside those buildings, you'd never know it existed. I bet those girls have no idea."

"They don't. I wanted you to see it...as a free woman."

"I'm free?"

"You're outside these walls. The truth is...you can run, I won't even stop you."

"I wouldn't get very far...not knowing how to swim."

"At least, life would be in your hands. There's no way they could take it back."

She nodded, gazing out at the sinking sphere. "The sun...I've never seen it so big. It's like I can reach out and touch it."

"That's an illusion, much like life."

"Some things must be real."

"Death, loss, sadness...they're real."

"Love is real," she said, staring at him.

He looked down, "Until it's gone."

"The woman I reminded you of...the one you loved, lost. Is that any less real today...than it used to be?"

He looked down. "Stop making sense. You're ruining my outlook on life."

She smiled. "The look on your face, in your eyes...when you mentioned her. That kind of love never dies...or so I hear."

"Some days I wish it would. The pain..."

"Can you tell me about her now? Since I'm a free woman for a few hours."

"She was so beautiful. Her skin so smooth, body so curved, hair so...red." He laughed, realizing something. "It sounds like I'm describing you."

"It does. The only difference...you *loved* her."

The two locked eyes, though he held back from confirming his feelings. He wasn't ready. "I did. She was murdered...along with our child."

"Child? Who could do such a thing..." she stopped in mid-sentence. "She was a slave. It's why you're here. This was never your choice."

He stared in her eyes. The pain explained it all. "Victor gave the order...had her killed. I was spared...to save others, break them down. Though, make no mistake about it. I died that day too. This is just...a shell."

Tears welled in her eyes. "You must believe...he's still in there. I see someone...so great. I see someone worthy of love. It'll happen again."

"A child...or love?"

"All of it...and more."

"No. My future's decided...and it doesn't include any of it. I mean, who'd love an old, broken, bitter man like me?"

She placed a hand on his. "I do."

She leaned in, kissing his lips. He pulled away, "I can't lose you...not the way I lost her. It's...happening again, the same as before."

Haley stood up, backtracking toward the wave-filled ocean. "If you won't have me...then the ocean will," she dared.

Bruce quickly stood. "You'll get all messed up...Victor will be furious. Besides, you can't swim."

"I guess you have a decision to make," she said, running into the water.

He flung his shirt off, revealing his concrete stomach. Running full force, he tried to catch her, though it was too late. She ran into the surf, engulfed by a powerful wave. He watched her red hair fly through the air, emulating the setting ball of fire.

Her silk nightgown clung to her body, hugging every curve. He froze, mesmerized by the sight. Suddenly, another wave crashed into her, sucking her into the undertow. Bruce dove into the water. A swirling sea clouded his vision, kicking up a sand-bed floor. Flailing his arms, he blindly searched, frantically cutting through the water. There was no sign of life.

As he emerged, she was nowhere to be found. "Haley!" he screamed, when suddenly, a pair of pale arms wrapped around his back. He spun around, as she slid to his front. Embracing his neck, she leapt into his arms, wrapping her thighs around his waist.

"Take me. Take me, now!"

"You'll get pregnant."

"*I know*," she declared, staring in his eyes. "I want your child inside me. Not Victor's. Impregnate me!"

Bruce's cock rose, realizing it was the one chance at capturing Haley's love. Thoughts of future consequence drifted to sea. Finally, he could reclaim the power from his captor. He had the chance to avenge his family's lives.

As Haley hung on, Mr. Knight lowered his pants. Lifting her higher, he placed her upon his bolder, hugged by her salty lips.

Her arms tightened around his neck, as she sank deeper onto his veiny manhood. The seawater increased the slickness, letting her move with ease. She gasped, feeling his bare flesh impale her tenderness. Having once sampled each other sexually, a rubber condom had denied skin upon skin.

The two held a collective breath, enchanted in newfound bareback bliss. Though, nothing could compare to the most forbidden prize of all: a kiss. Their virgin lips moved to each other like high tide to a lustful moon.

As a connection was made, another wave crashed upon them. The two disappeared, swept under the sea. However, it didn't faze them. Their salted tongues touched, lips lapped a sea of saliva.

The swaying current propelled Haley's body, letting gravity bob her upon Bruce's cock. Like a seductive siren, Ms. White's red hair flickered like a seaborne-flame, flowing like volcanic lava. Her flimsy nightgown hovered from her body, resembling an angel, fallen from heaven's grace.

Lost in their kiss, the two danced across 70-degree waters. They floated like ghosts, refusing to let their spirits evaporate. If another large wave hadn't crashed above them, they would've accepted death. However, nature's force evicted them from their mystical Atlantis. Propelled to shore, they slid into a bed of wet sand.

A waterfall trickled from their mouths, as their kiss remained unbroken. Battling the elements of earth, they refused to be unglued. Without parting mouths, Bruce's strong hands reached for the delicate nightgown. Tearing it in one slash, her wet skin was freed to press his.

Baked in body heat, they rolled in circles. Completely covered in mud, granules crept into every crack, bonded to each curve. Red hair turned muddy brown. For a moment, Haley gained control, riding her cowboy's cock like a prized mare. The sea's froth fizzed with her own, leaving separate trails of white upon the bareback journey.

Then, Bruce rolled her back over. Gripping her wrists, he pinned them above her head. Their smooth skin melted into one, as their joint body imprinted into earth. His thrusts picked up, forcing squirts of seawater from her vaginal crevasse.

The kiss finally ended. He chewed on her ear, licked her cheek, sucked her neck, and swallowed her full-breast. All the while, he drove deeper into her desirous dent. Haley's face tightened with pleasure, feeling a burning warmth inside her. Bruce's long cock tapped her womb, testing the limits of her cervix.

Timed with the setting sun, ocean winds picked up at their backs. With one last thrust, Mr. Knight exploded. A massive wave crashed, pooling beneath them. Flowing water stimulated their genitals, increasing all sensations. The cool ocean waters suddenly warmed, as Bruce's hot seed filled Haley's birthing canal. Ms. White shuddered in maternal ecstasy.

With each heavy squirt of life, the redhead continued to cum. She could feel it leaking inward. Haley counted each sperm cell slipping through her cervix. She stopped at one million.

A puddle of seawater formed their bed. Mr. Knight collapsed upon the breeder, as the two embraced. They both shed tears, unleashing pent up fears and captive frustration. To Bruce, it was the first time he'd cried since Carolina's death.

Tears kept flowing. Their hope laid in past lives reborn, present lives resurrected. Conception was far from guaranteed, though it was the closest to reality they'd ever come again. One way or the other, Haley had a date with destiny.

Unfortunately for them both, fate wouldn't be the only factor at play. Evil eyes scoured down upon them, watching their tryst from the guard tower. Tommy John's got more dirt than he could've wished for. If his plan worked out, Bruce Knight's rebirth would end in death.

*****

"You must hurry! We're going to be late!" Bruce yelled, watching Haley in the shower.

"I'm going as fast as I can!" she shouted, washing the mud down the drain. Her body sparkles went with it. So did her hairstyle.

"It's not fast enough! He'll have your head for this! Come out, now!"

Shutting off the water, Haley quickly stepped onto the tile floor. She dried off, looking worn and messy. "How do I look?"

Bruce sighed, realizing there would be trouble. "Fine. You'll have to go naked...there's nothing else."

"Then I guess...I'm ready," she said nervously.

"Go!" he said, leading her out. His watch showed, *8:01 PM.* He was prepared to take full blame, though had to think of an excuse. Any hint of sex would get them both killed.

*****

"What the hell is this?" Victor screamed in fury. Bruce and Haley remained silent, staring at him in fear. The Roman-styled red hair was currently a wet mess, and the nude body was of a slave, not a classy breeder. She didn't match the graceful setting before her.

A bed of carved snake wood was draped with hand-spun gold cloth. Two female slaves stood beside the bed, fanning it with palm leaves. A golden light filled the birthing suite, creating a sensual ambiance.

Bruce stepped up. "The blame lays with me, sir."

"Explain yourself! She should be sparkling like a spirit! Instead, she looks like a whore! A filthy slave!"

"I...took her outside the walls."

Victor filled with fury, as his open hand slapped Bruce's face. The humiliated Mr. Knight looked down, knowing better than to fight back. It was the first time Haley saw the strong man in a submissive role. He no longer looked like the guard in charge of her, but a fellow captive.

"You scum! Of all people...you know better than to risk such a thing! I asked you to take extra precaution!"

"You did."

"Then why the hell did you disobey me?"

He paused, opting to tell the truth. "She'd never seen the sea...I thought it would lift her mood."

"Oh...I'm *sorry*," Victor said in extreme sarcasm. "I didn't realize we're in the business of granting wishes."

"We're not," Bruce said.

"No shit!" Mr. Cruz screamed, smacking Bruce across the face again. This time he drew blood from the nose.

An embarrassed Mr. Knight let the blood slowly drip, as Haley looked away in sadness. "However you wish to punish me...just know it's my fault. If it means my death, so be it."

"No!" Haley shouted, suddenly realizing her mistake. Bruce shut his eyes in distress.

"Well...I see someone's got her attitude back," Mr. Cruz mocked. "Maybe I'll have her broken...correctly *this* time!"

Haley dropped to her knees in submission. "I'm sorry, sir...it's just...it's my fault. I asked him to take me...I jumped in the water. Punish me instead."

"She's lying," Bruce said. "I forced her out there...it's my punishment alone."

Victor cringed, realizing Mr. Knight had crossed a boundary. Although Cruz never suspected love or sex, he noticed something much more dangerous: *Compassion. If he cares so much for my breeder...then let him witness her brutal breeding.*

Approaching Haley, Victor gripped her arm extra hard. The redhead gasped, seeing the aggression in his eyes. He shouted, "This regal bed is not meant for a whore! You want to act like an animal? Then I'll breed you like one!" He grabbed her red hair, yanking her into an adjacent room. It was his backup plan.

Bruce stayed still, awaiting instruction. Before exiting, Victor shouted, "*You*...follow me!"

"Yes, sir," Mr. Knight said, entering the adjacent room. A proctology exam table was located in the center. It was basically a flat medical table, with an L-shaped knee rest at the end. There was no romantic lighting, plush bed, or hand cooled breezes to be found.

Victor made Haley kneel upon the L-shaped pad, laying her torso flat upon the table's bed. She formed a doggy-style position, ass cheeks in the air. Her hands were pulled straight, knees spread wide. Cuffs decorated the ends, waiting to be filled. "Knight...secure the breeder," Mr. Cruz said in cruel pleasure.

Bruce sighed, realizing they were both dead if he disobeyed. Moving into action, he refused to look at her. Instead, he locked her ankles into place. Heading to the other end, he cuffed her wrists. She was trapped. Her spread lips were offered to Victor like a lavish gift.

Victor yanked his pants down, unleashing his 8-inch, tanned cock. He stroked his swelling penis.

Sick with anger, Bruce asked, "Am I still needed here?"

"Oh *yes*. You're gonna be around for every moment of this. All 24-hours of her breeding," he insisted.

A gasp sounded from Haley, imagining the harsh length of time. Mr. Cruz approached her luscious lips. Placing his cock at her slit, he forced his way into her crater. There was no foreplay, romance, or care. In a way, it was like a male dog breeding his bitch.

Ms. White cried out, feeling his thickness enter her dry box. After a few joyless jolts, he paused. Reaching for her mouth, he ordered, "Spit!"

A few drops of saliva landed in his hand. He slapped her with it, yelling, "More, whore!"

Realizing he meant business, she unleashed an ocean into his hand. Withdrawing from her, he coated his cock in her lovely lubricant. He violently thrust into her, sampling a smattering of Bruce's remaining sperm.

As Victor withdrew, he witnessed a faint, whitish shellac upon his penis. He smiled, thinking it was a sign of her pleasure. "That's what I want to see!" he announced, having no clue of its ownership.

Bruce looked away, as his boss pumped the breeder from behind. He managed to block it out, as a loud smack reclaimed his attention. The spankings continued, as he drove harder and deeper into her.

Angry at her lack of reaction, Victor called out, "I guess you need the belt to get off. Knight...come here!"

The strong man tightened his fists, trying to withhold his anger. He forced himself to join them. "Yes, sir."

"Grab my belt...from my pants."

Bruce paused.

"Now, damn you!" Victor demanded.

Knight removed the belt, handing it to his boss. "Your belt."

"I won't be needing it. You will."

A silent sigh seeped from his lungs.

"After every inward thrust, you whip her ass cheek."

As he pulled back, Bruce failed to follow directions.

"Do it, damn you! I'll have you hung from chains again! Remember those days?"

Having no choice, the first lashing began. A rhythm was created. Each beating left a long red streak on Haley's pale skin. She fought the dual sensations for a while longer, before Victor got what he wanted.

The strong girl broke, crying out. Her pain threshold was crossed, again releasing her inner desire. With every landing of leather, chills crossed Haley's lush landscape. Hearing the tears mix with moans, Mr. Cruz's lust approached eruption.

Although Bruce's sperm had a head start, it would soon be outnumbered by the millions. Having no way to even the score, he had to hope that true love would be enough.

With one last thrust, Mr. Cruz grunted, firing a large load into Haley's fertile womb. Holding his hand up, he motioned for Bruce to stop whipping. Pretending not to notice, he hurled the hardest swing of the night, beating his boss's bare ass.

"Ahh!" Victor screamed, withdrawing before finishing. He continued squirting on the floor, rubbing his painful wound.

Although Haley couldn't see it, her tears stopped. A slight smile crossed her face, knowing Bruce got revenge for them both.

In a rage, Victor rose, yelling, "You damn ape! I told you to stop!" He pulled the belt from Bruce's hands, hurling the leather strap at Mr. Knight's body. Unlike his boss, he barely flinched. Victor tossed the belt to the floor.

He looked over at Haley's red bottom, focusing on trickling cum from her gaping hole. Rushing over, he pressed her folds shut, ensuring every drop would enter.

"Am I done?" Bruce asked.

"Stand over there!" he shouted, pointing at the back wall.

Things calmed, as 30 minutes passed by. No one said a word, as the two slaves entered the room holding a long, white baster. Victor took it from them, approaching the cuffed redhead.

Spreading her lips wide, he entered the clear plastic tube inside her. Pressing the plunger downward, a thick, white substance emptied into her. She squirmed feeling unthawed sperm slither through her birth canal.

Taken from Victor throughout the years, it was put into deep-freeze, ensuring survival. As it emptied, Mr. Cruz returned to his seat.

After another 30 minutes, another breeding session began. He called Bruce over, telling him to beat Haley. Nausea filled his stomach, as it was hard enough watching the man he hated, fuck the woman he loved. Beating her was just icing on the doughnut.

The pounding continued longer. In order to keep Haley stimulated, Victor activated a switch on the chair. A massive vibration shook, buzzing her resting clitoris. Her pressed breasts were also teased, jittering her nipples like jumping beans.

Exploding into forced orgasm, the added sensation pushed her over the edge again. Feeling her vagina constrict on his cock, Victor sent yet another load into her canal. The pattern repeated itself for 24-hours. Different stimuli were added to the scene: ice, heat compresses, multiple sized butt plugs, and a massive dose of Viagra for Mr. Cruz.

By the end, Haley lie motionless upon the buzzing chair. She was numb, red, and spent. Cum poured out like vanilla soft serve. Pulling up his pants, an exhausted Victor examined his strained cock. It was as bruised as Ms. White's behind.

He walked up to her. Leaning in, he shouted in her ear. "This could've been so right! Don't you see? When you disobey me, this is what you get! If you fail me again...it'll be a bullet," he said, staring up at Bruce.

Already running on adrenaline, Mr. Knight fought himself from tearing Victor apart. Instant memories of his beloved Carolina invaded his mind. He could feel her fallen body in his arms, dying from a bullet to the back.

Seeing the fire in Bruce's eyes, Mr. Cruz knew his message was sent. "Take her back to the room," he said, exiting.

Mr. Knight ran over, freeing Haley's wrists and ankles from the cuffs. Taking her into his arms, he tapped her face, trying to revive her. "Haley! Talk to me! Show me you're alive!"

Her green eyes opened at half-mast. A slight smile formed, quickly fading away. Lifting her in his strong arms, her head rested upon his broad chest. He hurried her back toward the room.

In the hallway, Tommy Johns awaited him. Looking at the defeated girl, he began laughing loudly. As much as Bruce wanted to discipline him, Haley's health mattered more.

"Congratulations to the expecting mother," Tommy announced.

As Mr. Knight disappeared from view, Mr. Johns' eyes grew hungry with opportunity. He said to himself, "In a few months...we'll find out who the real father is."

*****

Millions of Victor's sperm cells raced through Haley's cervix, into the uterus, and up the fallopian tubes. As the weakest died off, only a few hundred of the most ruthless reached Haley's matured egg.

Each possible heir was meaner than the next, fighting for a chance at fertilization. One in particular was the nastiest, rising to the top of the cream. It attempted implantation, only to find the egg already occupied.

Access denied.

Bruce and Haley's zygote held firm along the ovarian wall. It was strong, healthy, and ready to develop into an embryo. Though if Victor were to discover its genetic makeup, *that* opportunity would never arrive.

Part Three

Into the Fire

CHAPTER NINE

A helicopter's blades chopped tropical air, descending onto an island's white sands. Completely isolated from the world, nothing surrounded or occupied the protruding landmass. To a normal person with abnormal wealth, it would be the perfect place for a dream home. Though, to a power-hungry megalomaniac, it was just another brick in an empire.

The pilot exited the cockpit, sliding aircraft doors. A naked brunette slave leapt to the ground, forming a doggy-style position. A leather shoe followed, stepping upon her hardened back. Her hind muscles were particularly tight. If one looked closely, they'd see a permanent sole imprinted into her tanned skin. Unfortunately for her, no one looked.

The pilot reached out, offering a hand. "Mr. Cruz," he said.

Putting his full weight upon the slave's body, Cruz stepped down upon the granules. He smoked a fat cigar, vapors rising into hot air. Another female slave shadowed him with an umbrella, filtering an aggressive sun. A suited man followed him out, offered no such luxury.

"*Paraíso!*" Mr. Cruz announced, pausing to reflect upon the word. "No. One day...this could be the opposite of paradise. *Hell*. It's certainly hot enough."

"Is it to your liking, sir?" the suited man asked.

Cruz continued his silence, gazing at the endless blue moat trapping him in. Only waves made noise, hushing in a chorus of desolation. "We'd have complete autonomy?"

"I have Mr. Castro's word, sir. For the right price, this island will be free from Cuban rule...free from global eyes."

He waited another moment, finally nodding his head. "Hijo! Come here!"

A young child leapt from the helicopter, mercilessly landing on the kneeling slave's back. He merely repeated his father's actions. At such an impressionable age, every learned response molded him into a harsher human being.

Another female slave ran after him, carrying an umbrella to shield him from the sun. Refusing to stand still, he made her task difficult.

"Make sure he stays covered!" Mr. Cruz yelled at the woman.

The boy paused, letting his personal slave catch her breath. He looked around unimpressed.

"What do you think, hijo? Should we buy this big sandbox?" Mr. Cruz asked.

"I don't give a fuck," the boy said, continuing to run in circles.

A laugh of approval sounded from Mr. Cruz's throat. "Like father, like son."

Chasing him again, the slave slipped on the grainy ground, letting the hot sun discomfort the boy's skin.

"You bitch!" Mr. Cruz screamed, removing his belt. He went to beat the woman, causing her to cower into a ball. Right before striking her, he stopped. Looking over at his son, he said, "It's time you learned how to rule an empire. You decide. Do I beat this slave for failing you? Do I show mercy?"

The boy paused in confusion. He looked in her eyes, seeing pure fear. Having seen his father constantly beat women, he let instinct answer. "Beat her!"

A large smile crossed Mr. Cruz's face. "That's my boy!" He handed over his belt.

Taking it in his hands, fright took over the child. "I don't know how?"

"Do what comes natural."

The female slave stayed frozen in place, hoping for rare mercy. Fear tainted the child. Ordering a beating was obviously easier than committing one. Tapping into his emotions, he gripped the belt tightly. His small arm swung the leather strap. It was light, though hard enough to sting.

The slave cringed.

Mr. Cruz shouted in joy, letting pride explode from him. Tears filled his eyes, seeing the first sign of authoritarianism take root. To a man like him, it was more monumental than the child's first steps. Of course, he wasn't there to see them; the whipped slave was.

Feeling a newfound power, the boy smiled with pride. He flogged her again, creating a greater cry. Louder, raspier laughter sounded from Mr. Cruz. The lashings got harder, faster. Seduced by power, the boy aged in front of his father's eyes.

Tears fell from the slave's face, increasing the boy's craving for inflicted pain. It was a feeling of instant worth, providing a respite from his father's smothering shadow.

As the slave's skin started to break, Mr. Cruz reached out for the boy. "That's enough for now."

Ignoring his father, he continued the beating. He appeared to be possessed by pain's infliction. It only stopped when Mr. Cruz caught the belt in his hand. A surge of anger overcame him, as he began beating his son. The injured slave shielded him, absorbing the punishment.

After stopping, Mr. Cruz said, "A successful master knows when to kill slaves...and when to profit off them. She has worth to us...we'll use up every ounce of it. You'll learn like I once did!"

Kicking the slave in anger, the boy yelled, "Get up, slave! Shade me!"

The elder man was named Hector Cruz. He began laughing again, pulling his son close. Turning toward his suited companion, he said, "Tell Fidel, we'll take the island...any price he asks. Tell him, someday...it'll belong to my son. It'll belong to a man more powerful than he. His name is Victor! Victor Cruz!"

*****

A 40-year-old Victor Cruz reclined in his office chair. He gazed out the window, perched high above the ocean blue. Memories of his father were always present, though nothing was as vivid as the island's introduction.

He cradled a gold-dipped bullet in his hand. "I hope you're proud, papa," he said, closing his fist upon the spent .45 casing. If his father were watching, he'd be proud indeed. He'd also be seething with revenge.

Setting the example himself, the father couldn't blame the son. Hector constantly bragged about killing his own papa. He spoke with such pride, regaling each detail like cherished heirlooms. "At the end of the day...one man stood in my way. One shot...and I was king," Hector once told the boy.

Victor recalled his *own* golden moment. He was in his late teens, having invited his father for the island's groundbreaking. A large crowd watched, as he called the elder onto the stage, suddenly placing a gun to his father's head.

"What the hell are you doing?" Hector asked.

"Claiming the throne," Victor said coldly.

Shaking his head in defeat, a proud smirk crossed Hector's lips. "Like father, like son," he said, before a .45 ripped into his skull. The people watched in fear, witnessing the reign of a new king. He was more ruthless than the last.

Reclining further in his chair, Victor brought the bullet casing to his lips. Kissing it, he recalled watching the slave dig it from Hector's brain. He had it dipped in gold, immortalized as his trophy.

He wondered, *Will my heir do this to me? Or...will I take him out first?*

There was a knock on the door, causing him to tuck it away. Tommy Johns entered. "Sir. Can I speak to you...consequence free?"

"Just this once. Speak."

He paused. "We both know Bruce Knight is weak. He follows your breeder around like a lost puppy. With a few months until she give's birth, he'll return a pile of emotion. The men don't respect him. He's lost all ability to lead."

"Get to the point, Mr. Johns."

"I want to challenge him...for control. I want my old position back."

Victor paused in thought. "I replaced you once...used goods are not my style."

"I'll earn it!"

"How so?"

"By uncovering a lie so big...you'll return me to your side, sir."

"I'm listening."

"The baby is *not* yours."

Victor paused in total disbelief. "You dare insult me with your *own* lies?"

"Provable lies, sir."

"Pure speculation."

"I witnessed them with my own eyes. Knight fucked her...the night of her breeding...on the beach."

Victor's blood started to heat, though he pulled back. "Mr. Knight has been nothing but loyal. I don't believe he'd throw it all away for some...breeder. No matter how attractive."

"Put my word to the test, sir. I spoke to Dr. Gray...a DNA test is now possible. I'll be instantly vindicated."

"You realize if you're wrong...you're *dead*."

"Yeah. But the question is...what if I'm right?"

Victor went into deeper thought. "Take a man...bring her to the doctor. I don't want any messes made. This stays quiet...Bruce never knows. The heir is *not* to be harmed."

"Never, sir! But...how will I get her away from Knight? He watches her like personal property."

"Your accusation...your problem."

*****

Warm streams of water flowed from the showerhead, as Haley White ran a hand over her protruding belly. She was six-months into the pregnancy, and the days were getting shorter. *This is Bruce's child. I can feel it in my soul,* she assured herself.

Bruce was pressed against her wet back, wrapping her in his warm arms. The ridge of his nine-inch cock aligned with the curved crack of her ass. It fit perfectly, tucked snugly as if molded for each other.

Soft soap suds poured down her stomach and breasts, as his large hands traced her life-filled arch. Popping every bubble along the way, he felt the baby tapping inside. The fetus warmly acknowledged its true father's presence.

He pressed his face into her sopping red hair, inhaling the wet scent of freshly squeezed citrus. Nibbling upon her ear, he licked down her neck, drinking her like dry earth absorbing rain.

His hands glided along her full breasts, swelling with hormonal desire. Even his large grasp couldn't corral their heaving limits. He massaged them with slippery soap, stimulating her erect nipples. Her mammary glands filled with milk, though she had yet to experience lactation. In the early stage of production, it would take more than a gentle breast rub.

Bruce bent Haley over, feeling her cheeks tease his rigid offering. The slick trail of soap pooled in the gully, lubricating them both. Reaching around, he hugged her belly. She'd never felt more secure in her life.

He aimed his mushroom head at her creamy crevasse, feeling her soapy lips stick to him. The warm water drizzled like a sun shower, as Bruce gently penetrated his redheaded lover. Every inch of his spear slid inside, swallowed by her heaving heaven. It was so soft and creamy, Knight fought his urge to immediately soil her with masculine satisfaction.

Haley remained bent, held tightly while penetrated from behind. A rhythmic motion began, as if swaying to the calm tick of a metronome. Ms. White's canal stretched, fully adapting to Bruce's manly monument. He reached his cock's base, feeling his lover's soft innards milk his rod in sweet spasms.

The pace remained peaceful, as Bruce pumped her in thoughtful strokes. He used her round, feminine body to glide her back and forth. All the while, he continued to massage her swelling breasts.

Sliding his other hand to her clit, two fingers pinched hold of the engorged love button. Slick soap aided his smooth spin, stimulating her entire sex with a combination of arousing measures.

Haley's lips began to tremble, as her face tightened. She covered her own mouth, masking the moans. Sounds of sex were unsafe in such a place. Absorbed into her skin, lustful cries evaporated in the steamy air. Her body trembled in cold chills, tightening the birth canal in motherly fits.

Feeling her choke his spear, Bruce unleashed his white seed into her fully-grown garden. Pressing her breasts, he pulled her thick cheeks closer into him. Each seeping stream swam through her, nutritiously enhancing the fetus. The reminder of his baby inside her, made her glow with pride.

They collapsed upon the shower floor, steam rising from their skin. The hot water continued to boil them, as Haley placed her red head upon Bruce's broad chest. While Knight's thick load seeped from her pink slit, she licked down his defined stomach, arriving at his cock.

Her mouth encapsulated his cream-covered tool. Lines of cum still oozed from him, running down Bruce's shaft to his round testicles. She swallowed every sweet drop, reclaiming her remaining juices. Sucking all the way down to his balls, she felt his spent spear shrink upon her tongue.

Fully cleaning him of their shared offering, she rose back to his mouth. Engaging in a passionate kiss, they bathed in each other's leftover lust. As the kiss broke, Haley returned her head to his chest.

She let his heartbeat join in chorus with the soothing splatters of water.

After finishing, they dried each other with towels. Bruce got dressed, Haley stayed nude. For a moment, they could've been mistaken for an *average* couple on a Sunday afternoon. Certainly not captives. They even began to think of themselves in such a manner. The longer Victor stayed away, their caution lessened more. "What do you want to name the baby?" Haley playfully asked.

"I don't think *I'll* be consulted. In fact, I don't think *you'll* be consulted either."

"A girl can dream, can't she? What would you name the child? If it was ours to parent."

He thought. "Alyssa."

She smiled, "My middle name. You have a good memory. Though, that would mean it's a girl? Don't jinx me."

"Remember...we're dreaming. Mr. Cruz has no jurisdiction in *that* world. I want a daughter...a redhead, just like you."

Turning towards him, she placed her belly against his firm body. Staring in his eyes, they moved into each other's lips. Suddenly, the room's hall door opened.

"Who could that be?" Haley asked.

Bruce removed his gun, whispering, "No one I'm expecting."

Mr. Knight led the way out, seeing Dr. Gray and the nurse. The food cart had arrived simultaneously. "It's time to pump...test the quality of your breast milk," the doctor said.

"I was never told of this," Bruce said.

"Well, *I* was told...which is all you need to know," Dr. Gray scolded him.

"What are you gonna do to her?" Bruce suspiciously asked.

The nurse held up a breast pump. The doctor took it from her hands, addressing his patient. "Lay down on the bed."

Haley looked at Bruce strangely. They were both untrusting of the man, especially with him coming to her room.

Bruce asked, "Victor approved this?"

"You're free to check with Mr. Cruz...though, we'll be done by then," he said.

"Don't worry," Haley ensured him. "It sounds like something Victor would do. As long as you're here, I'll be fine."

Her pregnant form headed toward the bed. Bruce's cock overrode his worry, seeing the red haired beauty climb on all fours. She sprawled upon her back, getting comfortable in the satin sheets.

"Coffee?" the food cart slave asked Mr. Knight.

"Sure," he said, taking the cup from her. As Bruce sipped it, Dr. Gray snuck a quick peek. He quickly returned his attention to Haley.

Over the months, Mr. Knight became careless. The more time he spent with Ms. White, the less paranoid he became. Therefore, the less safe they were. When they weren't making love in the shower, they shared food and conversation.

Bruce was infected with the deadliest disease of all: emotion. It once put him in chains, leaving his lover's remains in a shallow grave. He took a bigger sip of coffee, sucking it down. His eyes remained on Haley the entire time.

The nurse pinched Haley's nipples, forcing them to the height of erection. She brought two separate tubes to the stiffened red bumps. At the tube's ends were thick, plastic tips. Each tube ran through small baby bottles, hanging directly underneath. Large suction cups attached onto her swollen breasts, creating enough pressure to force the nipples and aureoles deep inside.

The redhead gasped at the intense squeeze. "We begin," Dr. Gray announced, activating the first cycle. A fast sucking stimulation began, priming the glands.

Haley's body tensed, as the nurse held her down. "Relax, Ms. White."

"It's so...sensitive!"

"I'll take care of that," Dr. Gray announced. Reaching for a Hitachi Magic Wand vibrator, he turned it on. An intense buzzing filled the air.

"*What*...that..." Bruce slurred, unable to form a full sentence. Haley looked over at him oddly, knowing that wasn't normal. Beads of sweat poured down his head, as he ran a hand over his eyes, trying to stabilize himself.

A moan filled the air, as the redhead's attention was hijacked by a vibrated clitoris. The bulbous knob was placed on her wet, pink clitoris. The nurse spread the thighs and upper lips, letting the buzzing probe deeply stimulate the sensitive nerves.

The pump's fast cycle simultaneously sucked harder. Combined stimulations made her body shake with violent lust, forced into orgasm. Fully aroused, she tensed tightly, making every muscle work overtime. Cold chills crept across her skin, straining her nipples beyond their physical limit. Suddenly, small blasts of aerated liquid burst from her ducts.

Spraying like an aerosol, lines of motherly milk trickled down the tubes, collecting inside the bottles. Fast sucking air-blasts made her body tense more. Her aureole nerves sent tingles throughout, matching the pulsing waves emanating from her swelled clit. Liquid pleasure leaked from her upper and lower glands.

Suddenly, the air pump relaxed, entering the second cycle. It was slower, more of a tease than squeeze. Her orgasm also calmed, receding, therefore causing less milk flow.

Expecting those results, Dr. Gray gazed at the nurse. He nodded, as she reached for a syringe.

Bruce squinted his eyes, as the room slowly swayed. "No needle..." he barely managed to say.

"Are you, OK?" Haley shouted. "You don't look well."

"He'll be fine," Dr. Gray said, filling the syringe with a clear liquid.

"How do you know?" she asked in wonderment.

"Because, I provided the drugs in his coffee."

"No!" Haley shouted, as the nurse held her down. Bruce lunged toward the bed, dropping to his knees. The coffee cup fell from his hands, joining him on the floor.

Tommy and Rico entered, approaching him. Tommy spoke first. "Don't worry, she'll be in good hands. We're just gonna...borrow her for a while."

"Fucker!" Bruce managed to shout, fighting the dizziness.

"Will he feel this?" Rico asked, kicking Bruce in the ribs.

Mr. Knight's vision blurred in and out of focus. The scene before him spun though was clear enough. He fought to increase his pulse rate, forcing his heart to thump so hard it neared failure.

However, the results would push the drug faster through his system. It wouldn't be flushed, though good enough to regain a surge of strength. It wasn't working fast enough.

Looking back at Bruce, Rico was reminded of their last official meeting. "Switch off!" he requested. "I have something to finish."

Hacking laughter sounded from Tommy's throat. Withdrawing from the soaked vagina, they switched places. Rico climbed between Haley's pale thighs. Tommy shoved his cock deep into Haley's mouth, making her swallow recycled juices.

Warmth filled her, as she tingled in another world. Bruce watched in disbelief, seeing his love forced to enjoy his enemies. With every stroke, they tainted his child. A loud moan filled Bruce's ears, as Rico penetrated Haley's sphincter.

Her anal canal released all tension, allowing him easy access inside her. He thrust his eight inches into her dark cavern. As he hit his cock's base, he reached out for Ms. White's neck.

His second attempt at erotic asphyxiation was born. The first ended with Bruce pummeling Rico's face. Revenge was on Mr. Rain's mind, as his grip tightened upon her throat with each anal thrust. She gasped for breath, as Tommy's cock plugged her airway.

Haley's body shook with violent streams of forced ecstasy. Her vaginal juices bubbled from her seeping vulva, softening his anal attack. The harder Ms. White came, the more milk flowed from the breast pump.

A grin came to Dr. Gray's face, seeing the bottles fill to the brim. The milk began to overflow, reversing up the tube towards the nipple. It only increased the pressure intensity.

"Ay caramba!" Rico shouted. As he neared the emptying point, he squeezed harder on her throat. She choked on both Tommy's cock and Rico's hands. Right before she lost consciousness, Bruce rose from his induced coma.

Leaping onto the bed's end, he gripped Rico's neck, pulling him backwards. Thrown off the bed, Mr. Rains was forcefully withdrawn from Haley's anus. Crashing upon the floor, Knight conjured every ounce of strength, snapping Rico's neck. The scumbag was dead upon impact.

"You bastard!" Tommy shouted, removing his cock from Haley's mouth.

"Nurse...a sedative!" Dr. Gray shouted.

The nurse tossed it to him, as he ran at Bruce. Mr. Knight swept the doctor's knees, knocking him to the floor.

Even with the room spinning, he relied on vengeance to see. Bruce crawled for the syringe, as Tommy jumped upon Knight's back. They wrestled for control, though the more they rolled, dizziness became the ultimate enemy.

The doctor returned to his feet, injecting Mr. Knight with the sedative. Bruce crawled a few feet, collapsing to the ground.

"Rico!" Tommy shouted, turning his partner's head. Lifeless eyes stared back, as a line of blood dripped from his mouth.

"It's too late," Dr. Gray said.

"Scum!" Tommy declared, kicking an unconscious Bruce. He turned, kicking the doctor next. "I'd kill you...if I didn't need the DNA. Do it now, damn you!"

"Ok! Ok! Just take her to my office," Dr. Gray pleaded.

Tommy yanked the pumps from Haley's nipples, tossing her over his shoulder. Her dazed, pregnant body was carried out. An angry Mr. Johns gave Bruce one last kick. "How much time until he wakes?"

"I gave him a full shot...he'll be out for the rest of the night," Dr. Gray informed.

"Then if things go my way...he won't see the light of day," Tommy said angrily.

*****

"Lay her down here," Dr. Gray announced.

Tommy sprawled Haley upon the medical table. The nurse locked her feet into the stirrup cuffs.

Groggy, Ms. White began to come off the drug. She moaned, "Bruce."

"She's waking up," Tommy announced.

"Nurse, deal with it!" the doctor ordered.

"Already on it," the nurse said, placing a clear mask over Haley's mouth and nose. Turning a valve, gas began to flow. "I'll only put her in twilight...we can't risk full anesthesia."

"No!" Haley's weakened voice cried out, fighting her rolling eyes. Within moments, she drifted off.

Dr. Gray unveiled a long probe, encasing a hidden syringe. He lubed her used slit, working it deep inside. Meanwhile, the nurse held a scanner over Haley's pubic area. An image was beamed onto a screen.

The doctor used the image to guide the probe through the small cervical ring. Working it inside, he continued, until arriving at the fluid sac. Pressing the plunger, a small needle perforated the encasement. Dr. Gray pulled the plunger back, filling the inner syringe with amniotic fluid.

He carefully withdrew the probe, removing the syringe from within.

"How long?" Tommy asked.

"With *my* methods...I'll have paternity results within hours."

A smile crossed Tommy's face, as he stroked Haley's red hair. Leaning in, he whispered, "Bruce will be dead by tomorrow...as will *you*."

*****

Night fell upon the island. A muscular, ski masked guard had arrived from *Paraíso*. The man knew a few English words; patience was certainly one of them. He waited silently in front of Victor's desk. Mr. Cruz signed an order, sending a shipment of sex slaves to Venezuela. Business was booming.

They were interrupted by a frantic Tommy Johns. Dr. Gray calmly followed him in.

An angry Mr. Cruz lifted his head. "What the hell is this? You never barge into my office!"

"I'm sorry, sir. I've got news that can't wait," Tommy anxiously said.

"I'll decide *that*."

He handed Mr. Cruz a paper full of numbers. "The child's not yours! I was right...it's Knight's!" Tommy proclaimed.

The weight of 1000 steel knives sliced Victor's soul. "How sure are you? Any less than..."

"One-hundred percent!" Dr. Gray vouched. "I tested them against both sets of DNA. There are two certainties. One...the child is *not* yours. Two...it *was* fathered by Bruce Knight."

Having been with Dr. Gray since the beginning, Victor trusted him more than Bruce.

A moment of silence reigned, as the masked guard waited for the signed order. "I take?" the guard asked, while pointing at the signed paper.

Victor ripped it with his hands, translating with action. "There's a last minute amendment. *Pronto*," he told the man, holding his finger up.

Everyone looked around in confusion.

"Aren't we gonna kill the girl? Kill Knight?" Tommy asked.

"Mr. Knight dies tomorrow," Cruz said. "In fact, Mr. Johns...take Mr. Rains..."

"Rico's dead," Tommy said in sick anger.

"Compliments of the traitor?"

"Yeah," a shamed Tommy said.

"This guard, here...will assist you in tossing him to the dogs. It'll be just like the woman he loved."

"That honor belongs to *me* alone!" Tommy shouted, quickly adjusting his tone.

"You've already proven your inability to handle him. Shall I remove you from the task altogether?"

Shame covered Tommy's face, lowering his head. "Can I at least kill the bitch with my own hands?"

"She'll be spared...for the moment."

"But the woman carries his child!" Tommy argued.

A look of contentment crossed Victor's face. "A wise man once said...a successful master knows when to kill slaves...and when to profit off them. She still has worth. Make no mistake...the slave *will* pay for her actions. The slave *will* pay with her body."

CHAPTER TEN

Crack! Bruce was thrust into consciousness by a cruel whip. The building was of concrete, ground of sand, and air baked with humidity. He was hung from the ceiling by chains, feet dangling off the ground. *This is a nightmare! It's all just a nightmare!* He ensured himself.

"Die!" Tommy's voice yelled, while he whipped the prisoner's lightly scarred back. Knight was shirtless, though still wore the uniform black pants of the guard. The masked man from *Paraíso* joined him.

"This isn't real...it's only a flashback," Bruce shouted.

"Oh yeah? Does this feel like a flashback?" Tommy asked, as two whips lashed the back of his head.

Knight clinched his teeth in pain, refusing to break.

Laughter sounded from the shadows, though it wasn't Tommy's. Victor Cruz entered, dragging the tearful Haley by a neck-chain.

"Bruce!" a tearful Haley called out.

Victor smirked. "Good morning, Mr. Knight."

"Why the hell are you doing this? Why am I hung here again? Why is Haley in chains?"

"I see you're on a first name basis...though I suppose that's appropriate, considering you fathered her child," Mr. Cruz said.

Bruce gasped in shock, quickly covering for himself. "Bullshit! It's *your* heir...I was there when you sired it!"

"The game's up. I know about your treasonous night on the beach. I know that the child inside this *slave*...will soon be a bastard."

Shock filled his face, along with Haley's. Neither of them officially knew it was Bruce's. "A paranoid lie!" Bruce shouted.

"It's been tested, your word is officially dead to me. Your life will soon join it."

"Who told you this?"

"*I* did!" Tommy shouted, hurling the whip again. "I saw every fucking stroke."

Bruce pleaded with Victor. "You once told me...Tommy's just an opportunist! He's lying to you!"

"An opportunist...he *is*," Victor declared. "Though it's evident...you are something much worse. A traitor."

"You're making a mistake."

"No, Mr. Knight. The mistake was poisoning this slave with your DNA. She'll be the second girl you sentenced to an early death."

"No!" Bruce frantically shouted, kicking at Victor's unreachable face. "Kill me, spare her!"

"You know better than that. The man in chains never gets to negotiate. You die today."

"Bruce!" Haley cried. She ran for him, violently yanked back by the neck chain.

Victor smirked at the sight. "You should know...your slave...will die in a different way than you."

"How?" Bruce shouted.

"As a whore in *Paraíso!*"

Bruce tried to break the chains, straining himself to exhaustion. He couldn't do it, though refused to give in.

Victor continued, "She'll be kept alive...defiled, disgraced, used...along with the monster inside her. Her end may come from an overzealous asphyxiation or an unchecked VD. But know this...she'll earn back every cent you cost me."

Knight suddenly locked upon Haley's eyes. "You stay alive, no matter what happens! I'll come for you...I swear it."

Tears spilled from her, as her heart broke. "I know you will."

Mr. Cruz cut in. "Yet another tale he spins."

Bruce's cold, hard gaze turned toward Victor. "I'm coming for *you* too."

The confident smirk faded from Mr. Cruz's face, having seen that deadly look before. "It appears you'll never get that chance. Time is up, Bruce Knight," he said, turning towards Tommy and the masked guard. "Take him to the dog pit."

Tommy flashed his yellow teeth. He resembled a mutt nearing a garbage dump.

"Yes, sir," Mr. Johns said, as Bruce's chains were unlocked. He spilled to the floor, letting the blood flow return to his arms. Tommy and the masked guard unleashed a flood of whippings, drawing blood. "The dogs are gonna love you...like they loved your last redheaded whore!" Tommy mocked.

Bruce cringed, remembering Carolina's limp body being dragged.

Tommy forced Knight's black shirt back on. "Make the dogs work for their meal," he said, laughing in satisfaction.

Haley was dragged out by her neck chain, watched by Bruce the entire way. She was yanked out the door, headed for flight preparation. Although Mr. Knight made her a promise, they both knew it would take a miracle to keep.

*****

Victor reclined in his office chair, addressing Haley's guard. "Bring her to Dr. Gray. He's to package her for travel."

Although the order frightened the redhead, her concern was for Bruce. "Please, kill me instead! He's worth more to you...than a slave," she begged, dragged towards the medic wing by her neck chain.

Mr. Cruz exhaled, reclining further back. He couldn't erase Bruce's stare from his mind. *The last time I saw the kind of intensity...he took a life,* Victor thought.

A flashback played in his mind, taking him back to Mr. Knight's breakthrough training session. Although many years had gone by, it still serenaded his head like a catchy tune.

The scene in his memory was of Tommy and Rico, leading Bruce into the *expendable* slave-wing. Victor followed closely behind. The throwaway girls were temporarily moved, except one, who was caught spreading mutiny. She'd tried to talk the girls into attacking their masters. However, the slave facing Bruce was no master planner. She was just a scared young girl, nude and thin.

Mr. Knight's shoulder wound was patched up, bullet removed. His whipped back had barely healed, having spent a month in recovery, flat on his stomach. He was still in silent denial, swearing he wasn't like those men. The battle between good and evil raged inside his soul, and Victor was determined to push him over the edge.

Mr. Cruz led him toward the mattress. "This slave tried to escape. Even worse, she tried to enlist others in mutiny...the worst offense. It's up to you...to punish and break her. The harder you enforce the law, the more lives you'll save."

Fear painted the girl's eyes, matching Bruce's. She didn't speak English, though recognized the internal conflict on Mr. Knight's face. The look translated beyond words.

"How do I punish her?" he asked apprehensively.

Victor tossed a small rope at Bruce's feet, igniting the wicked laughter of Tommy and Rico. "Get creative."

Bruce hesitated, slowly bending to grab the rope. He knew the only way to punish her with it, would be around her neck. Victor knew the same.

Knight approached her, as she gasped. He stopped again.

"Fuck her first," Victor ordered.

"I'm really not in the mood," Bruce said.

Victor's hand quickly slapped Knight's face. "Haven't you learned by now? It's never about *your* mood...but my command! Deny me again, we'll just hang you back up. She'll be broken with or without you."

Knight exhaled. He dropped his pants, unable to conceal a 9-inch erection. Besides the forced blowjobs during his captivity, he hadn't penetrated anyone since Carolina. Moving toward the condemned slave, she tried to crawl away.

Quickly leaping into action, he grabbed her ankle. She was yanked to the mattress' edge, flipped over. He landed upon her, trapping the girl beneath his muscular body. Pinning her down by the neck, one thought raced through his mind. *I can't let others die like Carolina...no matter what it takes.*

Holding the rope in one hand, he held her soft neck with the other. Aiming his erect cock at her tight slit, he gently glided it in. It was an action the slave hadn't felt in a while. Most of the men she met, didn't know what gentle meant.

His eyes rolled feeling her tight, dry canal moisten with his advance. Although his grip remained upon her it never tightened to discomfort. It stayed at an aroused level. As her tunnel expanded, Bruce's thickness reached deeper inside her. He connected eyes with the athletic bodied brunette, infecting her with kindness. The act was turning into one of passion, fueled by his true nature, goodness.

Her legs voluntarily spread, wrapping around his muscular ass cheeks. She invited him in, forgetting all about her misdeed. A moan sounded from her, lost in the thickness stretching her thin frame.

"What the fuck are you doing?" Victor screamed, approaching the mattress. He kicked Bruce's backside, causing the man to withdraw. Knight's cock dripped with fresh slave juice.

"I'm following *your* orders," Bruce said.

Looking down at Knight's slick cock, Mr. Cruz ran a finger along the penis' top ridge, securing a sample of slickness. Holding the finger outward, he shouted, "*That* is the sign of pleasure! It's the opposite of what I commanded! You're rewarding her for running! Maybe I was wrong...hang him back up in chains!"

Tommy and Rico smiled, heading to restrain him.

"I'll break her," Bruce declared, banishing all goodness from his soul. It was the only way he could accomplish the task. Unfortunately, the only thing left to replace it was fury. The only fuel was his darkest memory. Once he let it consume him, he wasn't sure if he'd ever get his humanity back.

"Your last chance," Victor warned.

Bruce looked over at the reclined slave, then at the rope. He roughly grabbed her by the bony hips, flipping her face down. Forcing her into a doggy-style position, he gripped her hair.

Yanking back, he steadied himself, placing his bulbous head against her anal star.

Her own juices served as a light lube, as Bruce forced his way into her backdoor. The slave cried out, though it wasn't a new sensation. It was just more of what she'd gotten used to. It was the reason she ran in the first place.

He thrust deep into her dark cavern without pause. Pulling her hair back like a rein, he rode her like a wild horse. With each thrust, her head was strained more. However, it wasn't enough for Victor.

Mr. Cruz circled them like a school of sharks greeting an amputee. "Give-in to your anger. It's the only way to rule effectively. Think of the bullet tearing through your beloved slave, piercing her back...ripping the fetus apart!"

Bruce's thrusts became more pronounced, harder, merciless, angry. The fire in his eyes began to show.

"Think of her body tossed to the dogs...torn apart limb from limb! Why? Because *you* encouraged her to leave...like *this* whore did! She's as guilty for her fellow slaves as *you* were for killing the redhead!"

"Ah!" Bruce screamed out in personal pain, pounding his cock deep into the slave's colon. Sweat poured from his pores, sizzling upon his skin. His fist tightened upon her hair, nearing a ripping point.

"How far will you go to save others...so no one else has to die? Is the life of one...worth that of many? Punish her! Make her pay for her crimes! Transfer the hatred you feel for yourself...onto *her*!" Victor yelled, turning redder than the devil in a sauna.

A frantic Bruce let go of the slave's hair. Madness overtook him, as he reached for the nearby rope. Wrapping it around her neck, all thought emptied from his mind. The anal pumping continued, as he tightened it around her throat.

She began gasping for air, struggling for breath. Victor could see all humanity draining from Bruce's face. It was being replaced by darkness. With each pummeling thrust, the more he restricted her airway.

Reaching the height of fury, he finally broke. Buckets of sperm fired into her flaming flume. As he came, every vein swelled upon his body. His muscles tightened to stone. The rope reached its maximum velocity.

"Embrace the darkness, let it consume you! Let it *become* you!" Victor shouted in Bruce's face.

A desperate gasp sounded from the slave, as her body trembled in violent, forced orgasm. It was so intense, she stopped fighting, willingly crossing the boundary of life itself. Bruce felt her body go limp, dropping upon the mattress.

Withdrawing from her, he flipped her back over. He shook, seeing her eyes slowly open. "No!" he shouted.

"She's been broken," Victor said in satisfaction. "In fact, I can assure...she'll never do it again." He addressed Rico. "Put her body on display...hang it high, so her friends see what happens when you fuck with Victor Cruz."

Rico approached her, interrupted by a frantic Bruce. He opened her mouth, administering CPR. Fueled with adrenaline, he kept blowing, pumping life inside. He gave out from breathlessness, only achieving a more lifeless stare.

Victor leaned down, softly taunting Mr. Knight. "You killed her Bruce. Your hands took her life. It appears...we're not that different, after all. Welcome home."

"You fucker!" he screamed, tearing through the large room. He ripped a few mattresses to shreds. Next, he punched holes in the solid walls. Smashing anything he could get his hands on, he lost his mind.

"Should we put him down?" Tommy asked Victor.

"No. Like the slave, he's dying too. It's just on the inside."

After exhaustion overtook the broken man, he dropped to his knees, trembling in a human ball. The last of his human emotions emptied before Mr. Cruz's eyes. Victor approached him, leaning inward. "You are one of us now. Bruce Knight is dead."

The flashback always ended at that point. Returning to the present, Victor reclined further back in his leather chair. Although he hated to lose such a powerful tool in his empire, such betrayal had to be dealt with harshly. The only acceptable punishment was death.

*****

Haley was dragged to Dr. Gray's office, as the neck chain was released. Seeing tears stream down, the nurse comforted her. "Don't worry, Ms. White. This will all seem like a dream." She prepared a sedative.

"No," the doctor proclaimed. "Victor said not to waste chemicals."

"Just bag her? Without medicating her?" the nurse asked.

"She'll be tied, immobile."

"If not kept calm...she'll go mad from claustrophobia," the nurse said, reaching for a roll of thick gauze. "This is an old fashioned sedative from back home. Wrapped around her nose and mouth, it'll allow enough air for survival only. Though, the constriction will weaken her to the point of natural sleep."

A smile came to Dr. Gray's face. "Like a forced coma."

Panic filled Haley, hearing their plans for her. However, they paled in comparison to her fear for Bruce. Knowing it could get her killed, she decided to risk it all. *If Bruce dies, then life isn't worth living anyway.*

The doctor and nurse turned their backs to the patient, preparing the gauze gag. Without hesitation, Haley leapt off, breaking away quicker than an amniotic sac. By the time her captors noticed, she escaped through the door.

"Get her now!" Dr. Gray yelled.

*****

"Move pig!" Tommy shouted, accompanied by *Paraíso's* masked guard. He kicked Bruce in the back. The captive's hands were bound at the front, legs chained together. Mr. Knight fell face first on the pavement. "Get up!" Tommy Johns grabbed Bruce by his dark hair, yanking him back to his feet.

"You better hope I die," Knight threatened.

"You'll be prime rib to those Pit Bulls. I didn't see it myself, though Rico told me. The night your whore died, she was still alive when they ate her flesh," his raspy laugh sounded. "She felt every bite...like you will."

Fury overtook Bruce, as he lunged his chained body at Tommy. Both men spilled to the ground, as the masked guard pulled Mr. Knight off. Johns unleashed his gun, as the masked guard warned. "Victor say...no kill!"

"Just a flesh wound...in the shoulder," Tommy said wickedly.

"Bruce!" Haley's voice echoed in the distance.

"Haley!" Bruce shouted at the top of his lungs.

Dr. Gray and the nurse were also heard. "Help! Escaped slave!"

"Fuck!" Tommy shouted, putting his gun away. He pointed straight ahead, directing the guard. "To the pit! Wait to kill! I'll return!" He emphasized his words slowly and loudly.

The ski-masked guard nodded, remaining somewhat confused. He got the basic gist, yanking Bruce by his chained hands. Tommy ran towards the doctor's voice, following the sound.

"Haley...run!" Bruce shouted, though his lover's voice only grew more distant. He thought hard, thinking of a quick plan. An idea struck him. Making a similar move on the masked man, he barreled into the man's chest.

The guard had a gun already waiting, bashing Bruce over the head. Knight quickly went down, knocked out. Continuing the task, the guard dragged the unconscious prisoner to the pit.

*****

Haley ran toward the breeder's suite, remembering the emergency exit Bruce showed her. She arrived at the door, opening it. Anticipating her direction, Tommy blocked her like a brick wall.

She crashed into him. He trapped her in his arms, roving her nude body. Kicking at his legs, she tried to break free. Having no luck, she bit his hand.

Laughter sounded from him. "To men like me...that's foreplay."

Haley quickly stopped, as the doctor and nurse arrived. Struggling for breath, Dr. Gray said, "Thank you. I couldn't imagine explaining that to Mr. Cruz."

"I'll take her back...make sure she doesn't get away. Then, I'll go kill her man," he said, biting on her neck.

"Let me go!" she said in tears, realizing she failed Bruce.

Haley was returned to the exam room. Her wrists and ankles were bound. Tommy held her down, as the nurse wrapped the thick gauze around mouth and nose. Her breathing was labored, as evidenced by the rapidly inhaled cloth.

"Relax," the nurse said. "At first, it'll be scary. You'll feel like you're suffocating...but you're not. It'll slow breathing, make you sleepy...though keep you alive."

Although Haley ignored the advice, she eventually had no choice. Calming her inhalation, she began to take measured breaths. Weakening took over, as an overwhelming tiredness overtook her body.

The nurse gently reclined the bound beauty upon the table. The harder she fought to breathe, the weaker she got. Her eyes began to get heavy, as a natural sleep crept closer.

Wicked lust filled Tommy's eyes, equaling the drool in his mouth. His calloused hands roved her curves, arousing him to defile her again. However, a greater prize awaited him. "Is it done?"

"One more step," Dr. Gray said, aroused himself. He unleashed a large white sack, enough to fit a pregnant woman. "To protect her in transport."

Haley's eyes fluttered, fighting to remain open. Tommy and the nurse pulled her up into seated position, as she was encased like precious merchandise. Fully bagged, the sleepy beauty was laid back down. The bag was tied at the bottom, officially making her cargo.

"She's ready to go when you are," Dr. Gray said.

"The plane's being prepared now. Transport her to the runway. I have to finish Bruce Knight."

*****

The masked guard arrived at a thirty-foot concrete pit. Unlike its Venezuelan counterpart, the island's depth only went so far. Therefore it had to be re-enforced with the solid coating.

As the masked man leaned over the edge, four dogs leapt up at him. Their powerful jump was impressive, gaining 6-feet in the air. It was not enough to scale the wall.

Their bark was a fierce roar, though nothing compared to their bite. Jaws of death snapped like a steel bear-trap, yielding the PSI of

250. One bite could kill a man, though they were trained not to kill, but slowly devour. Having been starved for a day, they were anxious.

"Ruff!" the guard shouted, riling up the dogs in a taunting motion. "Perro sucio," he cursed them, spitting downward. As he leaned over, a rolling force suddenly swept his feet.

He screamed, tripping forward into the pit. Right before falling, he reached out, grabbing Bruce's leg chains with him. Pulled downward, Bruce managed to catch the wall with his bound hands.

The masked guard grabbed hold of his prisoner's legs. Dangling before the hungry beasts, one of the Pit Bulls caught the guard's foot. It chewed through the leather. Kicking the dog into the wall's side, a sharp squeal sounded. The animal fell while the others immediately took its place.

Bruce's muscles bulged, as he pulled himself to freedom. The guard climbed his prisoner like a human ladder, wrapping his arm around Knight's neck. A race to the surface began. Feeling the masked man overtake him, Bruce flung his head backward. Smashed in the nose, the guard fell again, catching Bruce's legs.

With a frantic upward thrust, Knight's body reached the surface. Rising with him, the guard grabbed the pit's edge. Free of the enemy's hold, Bruce wrapped his wrist chains around the opponent's neck. Squeezing tightly, a choking sound filled the air.

"Keys!" Mr. Knight demanded.

The frantic guard reached downward to his belt, holding on with one arm. He tossed them to Bruce. "Release!" the guard's accented voice strained.

"As you wish," he said, stomping the enemy's hands, dropping him into the pit. As the man fell, Bruce peeled the black mask off. It slipped off the guard's head into Mr. Knight's custody. Without it, his ultimate plan would never work.

A blood-curdling scream sounded as the ferocious Pit Bulls seized their dinner. First they feasted upon his exposed face, clearing every ounce of visible identity. Once he was unrecognizable, they butchered the rest of him. It was a fact Bruce counted on. To the average eye, Mr. Knight was dead.

He unlocked the cuffs from his wrists and ankles. Tossing them into the pit, they were returned to their owner. Taking a deep breath, he knew the monumental task that waited. Officially on borrowed time, one mistake would be his last.

Bruce slipped the ski mask on, already wearing the same black uniform. Seconds later, Tommy arrived. Noticing the human scraps, he shouted, "You foreign fuck! I told you to wait!" The metallic scent of blood hit his nostril, making him hunger for revenge. Bruce remained silent. He blankly stared back, ready to defend himself if necessary. Though, he hoped he wouldn't have to.

"What good are you damn people?" Tommy shouted. His attention was quickly diverted to the dogs devouring of the faceless man. A smile came to his face. "At least I didn't miss the best part."

Bruce quietly exhaled, hoping the *best part* was yet to come. He'd escaped imminent death, though was headed back to the place his life ended. Into the fire, he was returning to *Paraíso*.

CHAPTER ELEVEN

Bruce Knight's heart pumped in cardiac fury. Luckily, the black mask didn't reveal emotion upon his face. Sickness and anger merged, as he watched a bagged Haley carelessly carried over Tommy's shoulder.

Her body was limp, visibly unconscious. The curvy girl's outline was sharply defined, highlighting her nude pregnant form. Tommy Johns approached Victor, who watched the scene with a sense of regret. In the span of a day, he'd lost a powerful ally and a prime-breeding vessel. With every year that went by, his chances of an heir were fleeting.

"I'm assuming Mr. Knight is dog food by now?" Victor said.

"At this moment...he's already dog shit," Tommy quipped.

Victor nodded, accepting reality. He learned from his father to never form an attachment to anyone, since they're the ones who'd betray him. The lesson was proven true. "Then I congratulate you, Mr. Johns. You return to my favor again."

A look of satisfaction painted Tommy's face. "I'll load the slave on the plane now."

"Wait," Victor told him.

The masked Bruce listened closely, remaining a silent presence.

"Sir?" Tommy asked.

"Load her into the cargo bay. It's a tight fit, but she'll survive."

Knight's heart thumped harder, as he watched a small compartment open in the private jet's side. Any baggage was pushed aside, making room for new cargo. Tommy shoved Haley into the tight, dark space. He closed and locked it, wiping his hands.

Bruce restrained himself from going ballistic. Surrounded by multiple armed guards, he could take one of his enemies down, though be killed before striking the other. At that point, Haley would truly be hopeless.

Victor joined Tommy's side one last time. "I'll arrive in a few weeks, do inventory...clean house. Any slave not making money...will be liquidated. We're doing well, though growing too big...too many mouths to feed."

"I'll await your arrival, Mr. Cruz."

"Remember, now that you're back on top, the responsibility falls upon your shoulders. I hold you fully responsible for the redhead's obedience and performance. Any problems...I'll have both your heads."

"Yes, sir," he said, turning toward the concealed Bruce. "Go!" Tommy pointed at the plane, as Knight nodded, playing the foreign role. The two men approached the plane's cabin.

Bruce stopped before entering, taking one last look at the island. *I'll never see this place again. I'll either leave Paraíso with Haley...or die trying.* He looked down at Victor, who caught the masked man's gaze.

Mr. Cruz noticed something in the guard's eyes. It was familiar, yet threatening. Victor nodded in farewell, as Bruce nodded back. There was no doubt...they'd meet again.

*****

The plane landed upon the private runway. Tommy and Bruce exited the aircraft, inhaling a familiar scent. It had been a while since their return. *"Paraíso,"* he announced to a silent Bruce. Johns showed rare emotion, having once entered the country a broken man on the run from Interpol. Willing to do anything for shelter, Victor was happy to oblige.

The masked Bruce remained near as an aide welcomed them. "President Maduro sends his greetings. He is preoccupied at the moment. Squashing dissent takes time...you understand. He wishes he could come in person," the aide said.

"I don't need his greeting. I just need to know...will we get the same *royal* treatment from him, as we did under Mr. Chavez?" Tommy delivered Victor's question.

"You can count on it," he assured.

"That's all I needed to hear. Mr. Cruz sends his regards and condolences for your deceased leader. A true man of the people."

Bruce rolled his eyes at the statement. Anxiously waiting for Haley to be freed, he desperately wished to tear the plane's cargo doors off. Knight was silent during the entire flight. All he thought about was the vulnerable girl.

"Open her up!" Tommy shouted to the crew. They opened the hatch, revealing the shrouded redhead. She was dead still. Mr. Johns shook the body around, copping a feel. He felt a puddle at her crotch, acknowledging urination. "Wonder if she's even alive?" He pulled out a knife, causing Bruce to crowd him. "Back the hell up!" Tommy ordered. "She's mine."

Knight obeyed, as Tommy slit the bag open. The nude redhead spilled out. She was paler than usual, her body looked void of life. Bruce froze in fear, swearing to himself, *If she's dead, it all ends here. I'm going out in a blaze of glory.*

Tommy Johns unwrapped the gauze, allowing normal airflow to enter her nostrils. She still remained lifeless, as he checked her pulse. "Nothing." Bruce approached Haley again, crowding Tommy's side. "I said back off!" Tommy shouted, assuming the guard didn't understand.

Ignoring the warning, Bruce placed a hand upon Haley's lower breast, touching her heart. Suddenly, she frighteningly gasped, inhaling a deep breath of air. Her calm broke, jolting the frightened girl to life. She shook in confusion.

"She must like you," Tommy joked, shoving Bruce aside. "Welcome home, whore!" He pulled her from the flying tomb, thrusting her over his shoulder.

Mr. Knight kept his distance, as they approached *Paraíso.* An eerie feeling came over him as he looked toward the forest where Carolina died. He still saw her there, inside his arms. The horrid heartache that once plagued him, returned in full. After leaving Venezuela, he went to the island and never left.

Removing his gaze from the forest, he restudied the brothel. It had grown, along with business. Once Hugo Chavez took power, he took a special shine to the place. A popular whorehouse before his rule, it rose to legendary status during it. It was constantly crawling with global celebrities. They felt comfortable within the man's iron bubble, as long as they didn't have to live under it.

The building had been enhanced since his last visit. Built higher and wider, it was easily the largest *Gentleman's Club* on the planet. Bruce took a deep breath as a whole new set of challenges were about to face Haley and himself.

*****

Inside, Tommy handed her to another guard. Haley craned her head, taking one last gaze at the masked man who revived her. Mr. Knight was stopped at the door, ordered to rejoin his brethren. Lucky for Bruce, he understood Spanish better than he spoke it.

Trying to recover from the hellish plane ride, Ms. White had a moment to think. *That guard's touch...it felt just like...no, don't do this to yourself. He's dead,* she thought. Tears spilled down her cheeks.

She was brought into a room of 12 other pregnant girls. It was in the building's rear, hidden from the glitz and glamor. The seedy place had drab walls, harsh lighting, and small bunks. Much like her arrival on the island, it was a quick introduction to paradise's antonym.

Haley was returned to a standing position, left by the guard without instruction. Hearing the other girls, it was obvious few spoke English. Most were of Hispanic and Eastern European descent. Looking around, she didn't know which bunks were taken and which weren't. She began to cry, watched by everyone.

Suddenly, a voice sounded from behind her. "I got ya, mate...you're not alone," a blond girl name Sydney Riley touched her back. The scared redhead turned, seeing two faces she could relate to.

"We know exactly how you feel," said a darker blond Canadian, Charlotte Reed.

Haley lunged at the equally pregnant girls, embracing them in fearful shaking. "Thank you! Thank you!"

"Come on. Let's get you to a bunk," Sydney said. Leading Haley by the hand, they took her to a neighboring bed. "My name is Sydney, though they call me Syd. Well, *she* call's me Syd, since no one else understands us."

"I'm Charlotte...or Char."

"I'm Haley," she said, trembling. "I can't do this." She broke down in tears.

"Relax, sweetie," Sydney comforted. "I promise, it gets easier...when you accept the current situation. Note the word current...it's not forever. Not if I can help it. Anyway, I remember you from the island."

"Me too," Charlotte said. "Hard to forget. Red hair...deeper than the Canadian maple...flag, that is. The way you were called out of line, I thought you were a goner."

"Some days...I wish I was," Haley said. "I'd join *him*." She broke down again.

"Who?" Charlotte asked.

"*Bruce*. He's...*dead*," Ms. White said, placing a heavy hand upon her stomach.

"I heard that name on the island too. Wait...was he the man that trained us?"

"He was...but he's not like them."

"They're all the same," Charlotte said. "Good riddance."

"Not him! He has a good heart...good soul. At least, he did when he was alive." Haley shed more tears.

Sydney cut in, trying to ease the newbie's mind. "We all wanna die sometimes, honey. You have to believe your man survived...that we'll all escape someday. It'll destroy you otherwise."

She nodded. "You're right. He promised to come for me...no matter where I am."

"Do you believe in him?" Syd asked.

"With everything inside me."

"Then dry your tears, mate. He'll come."

Charlotte shook her head, refusing to fool herself with hopeful lies. "How far along are you...prego?"

"Over six months. You?"

"About four," Charlotte said.

"How'd you guys get pregnant?" Haley asked. "In training they warned us not to."

"We were chosen for a new project...pregnant prostitutes," Sydney said.

Charlotte rolled her eyes. "Losers...*ahem*, I mean customers paid for the privilege. I had no intention of having children...ever. If I'd known...I would've just told the guard member to drop his load. At least, his face was behind a mask. I could've pretended it was Tom Cruise...instead of Tom Green."

"Guard?" Haley asked. "You had sex with a guard?"

"Thursdays," Sydney cut in. "The night guard in charge...has an agreement with his men. They bang the lot for free...no one tells. Last week...our group was chosen. Judging on how quickly they finished, I'd say we're due for another round."

Haley looked shocked, though her mind was still on their pregnancies. "What will they do with your babies afterward?" Ms. White fearfully placed a hand on her own stomach. She remembered what Bruce told her about breeder children.

"We try not to think about that," Sydney said. "We really don't know."

Charlotte spoke passionately. "They better take the damn thing away. My luck...it will look like Bob and Doug Mackenzie's bastard child."

"Who?" Sydney asked.

"Strange Brew...a Canadian thing. Just stick to Vegemite."

"What's Vegemite?" Haley asked.

"It's an Australian thing...stick to peanut butter," Sydney said, continuing the chain of national pride.

"Anyway...they can toss this baby out with the enema water," Charlotte proclaimed.

"Char!" Sydney said. "You don't mean that."

"Nothing like a little honesty to lighten the mood, eh?" Charlotte asked.

"Well, if things go my way...I'll be free by then," Sydney said, lowering to a whisper. "In fact, I just might give it a go...sooner than later."

"Don't tell me you believe that crap story," Charlotte said. "Don't fill red's head with *that* BS!"

"I absolutely do believe it!" Sydney answered. "One of the Brit slaves told me. She heard it from another...down the line. You see, many years ago...a woman escaped through the woods, heading West. She made it into Columbia...to freedom!"

"Tell her about the other rumor," Charlotte said.

"She doesn't want to hear that."

"I do," Haley said.

"Ok, but I warned you. Anyone caught trying to escape goes down into a dungeon. It's a dark place underground, worse than hell. That's if you're not shot first, like the other girl."

"Other girl?"

"A customer and slave fell in love...they tried to escape into those same woods. The girl was shot in the back...thrown to dogs. The man was enslaved...trained to kill other slaves. Or so they say. I'd prefer to believe the other rumor."

"The slave...was she a redhead?" Haley asked intently.

Both girls' faces crinkled in wonderment. "I don't know," Sydney said. "Does it matter?"

"It does to me," she said cryptically, remembering Bruce's story about Carolina.

"I say they're both bullshit," Charlotte argued. "Look, this place isn't the border at Niagara Falls...they guard this place like a war zone. They're armed to the teeth. My advice? Forget any fantasies of escape, and just do the deed we were kidnapped for."

"How were you taken?"

"An Au pair job...in Switzerland, of all places," Sydney said. "It was a fake ad on the internet."

Charlotte cut in, "A bondage club. I was hired to show off my...whipping skills. I was hooded, rushed out the door, thrown into the back of a van. How were you taken?"

Before she could answer, a loud speaker interrupted them.

Suddenly, an announcement sounded over a loud speaker. It was in both Spanish and English. "Preparar. Prepare."

"Prepare for what?" Haley asked.

"To go to work," Charlotte said.

"Just follow us," Sydney instructed, as the three, nude pregnant women ventured into a large bathroom. They were joined by the ten other pregnant slaves. A man handed out thin bars of cheap soap. "Scrub the pussies good!" he shouted. The girls made their way to a line of five showerheads.

Haley followed along, as groups of three crowded together. A stream of cool water spit out, as Sydney and Charlotte washed each other. The two blonds lathered their breasts, backs, and cracks. They ventured deep inside their canals, soaping them up. Bad hygiene led to worse outcomes.

Ms. White watched them in shock, standing outside the water stream. Her mouth dropped open, watching each girl penetrate the others innards with soap. Gazing around, all the other's were doing the same. Each pregnant body was groped, covered in bubbles.

Sydney called out, "Mate, you better give this a go. We only get five minutes until the water's off."

Haley exhaled, joining her new sisters. She squeezed between the two, trying not to brush their intimates.

Charlotte was quick to correct her. "Red, don't be shy around here. Trust me, this is the least sexual contact you'll make all night," she said, shocking Haley.

Realizing she had to give in, she snuggled into place. Their soft, pregnant bodies pressed against each other, forming a curvy mass. Both girls lathered up. Sydney's soft hands gently lathered Haley's pale breasts, bringing her nipples to their peak.

Charlotte washed Ms. White's back, slowly running her soapy hand down the spine. As she slid in between the curvy cheeks, Sydney's hand delved into the velvet lips. Both girls got on their knees, penetrating both holes with their soapy fingers.

Haley started to tremble, desperately trying to fight an embarrassing orgasm. However, the deeper their double penetration went, the hotter she got. The cool water rained down upon her soap-soaked clit, slapping at it.

The girls' swollen fingers went deeper into the joint tunnels. Haley gripped onto Sydney's wet hair, unintentionally squeezing a fistful with each thrust. Adding a second finger, they filled the redhead's red flume with floral scents. Reaching their knuckles, they spun the doubled digits in small circles, scrubbing the inner walls.

Switching between slick thrusts and circular teases, anal and vaginal nerves were set aflame. Haley was so wet with her own juices a flood of soap began to seep from her soft holes.

Haley's bottom lip began to curl and tremble, as she bit down upon it. As hard as she tried to fight the cleansing, she broke in unwelcome orgasm. Her moan echoed off the tile, as the others just went on with their business. It was a typical day at the office.

Syd and Char also continued-on like professionals, having seen and done it before. Desensitized to the act, they all had their moment of humiliating pleasure. They kept pumping her, making her orgasm continue.

Her thighs trembled, as she tried to choke the invaders. Knowing it was better to finish her than stop midstream, Syd and Char picked up their speed and intensity. While their fingers flowed like fireflies, Sydney brought her free hand to the soap-covered clitoris. Pressing inward, she spun in a tornado of teasing.

The mother orgasm arrived, as clearly the other's were just preparation. Haley's moans kept escaping, as her nipples swelled, breasts shook, and legs weakened. Held up by the girls, she finally calmed. Her face was redder than her hair. "I'm so embarrassed."

"Relax, sweetie," Sydney said. "You're just human...like us all." She washed the residue away. Haley took another rinse, needing to cool herself off. The water flow ended, as the male assistant shouted. "It's time for your enemas."

"Enemas?" Haley whispered.

The two nodded, moving into place. They lined up against a trough with a drain at the bottom. Each girl bent over like a drinking horse.

Snapping on a rubber glove, the man spread the first slave's butt cheeks. Lubing it with a glob of goo, he went from one hole to another. Afterward, he administered the first enema. He used a double-barrel fleet enema in both holes, rinsing them anally and vaginally. There was a separate one for each girl.

Haley's heart thumped wildly, awaiting her turn. As he went down the line, the veterans took it like champs. Getting one every day, they were used to the heavy feeling.

Haley's turn came, as she tensed up. Sensing her newbie fear, the man pushed the tubes to their limit. Finally satisfied, he unleashed the saline wash. She trembled as her innards frantically filled. Both canals swelled with fluid, entering the depths of her body.

Finally finished, he moved on. Haley shook, trying to hold it in. "What now?" she whispered.

"We wait until we're told to empty," Sydney said.

"Where?"

"Look down," she said, gazing down at the trough drain.

Haley gasped. Another ten minutes expired before the assistant said, "Expel!"

The girls stood up, turning around. They squatted over the rectangular trough. Haley was humiliated, though relieved to let go. Each girl held onto their neighbor, holding themselves up.

Once fully emptied, they were towel dried. A separate slave did their hair and makeup, ensuring they'd look classy for the customers. There was no need for clothes, adding to the sexual allure.

The man shouted, "Alienation! Line up!"

The girls quickly headed for the door. Sydney, Charlotte and Haley were next to each other.

"Where we going?" Haley whispered, following their march.

Charlotte didn't waste words. "Just smile and look pretty. Then, get ready to fuck."

*****

Mr. Manuel Correa entered the showroom. Decked out in Versace, he matched the marble floors and walls. The room was used for all the lineups, glowing with tones of red and gold. An ambiance of sex was ever-present.

The well-dressed man walked down the slave-line. Although he was a VIP, having spent hundreds of thousands there, he'd never sampled the pregnant girls. He examined each of their curved bodies like cattle at auction. Each breast was squeezed, vagina plunged with his finger. Unable to choose, he said, "I'll try them all."

Tommy joined the attendant, keeping a close eye on Haley. He made sure she didn't shame Victor's reputation with insubordination.

The attendant's eyes lit up. "Most excellent, sir! Would you like the regular room...or do you care to try our theme rooms today?"

"It's been a while...let me see the themes again."

"Yes, sir. Follow me. Girls," the attendant pointed, ordering them all to follow.

*****

They ascended red-carpeted stairs, looking more like *Gone with the Wind* than a whorehouse. Along the way, Haley studied her new surroundings. She was struck by the stained-glass windows stretching the lobby walls. The closer she looked, she realized each character wore Victor's face. That included the godly figure with beams shooting from his hands.

As they arrived on the second floor, an array of women were scattered around. *There must be thousands of slaves here,* Haley thought. *We outnumber the guard ten to one. Why don't they ever revolt?* She looked down at a guard's gun, suddenly realizing why. Unarmed, they had no chance.

Stopping at each room, Manuel reacquainted himself with the different themes. Haley peeked inside. There was a room to cater every fetish. The water-sports room was covered in tile, multiple drains at the floor. A nude Hispanic girl lay flat, urinated on by three men.

Haley gasped, hurrying to the next one. There was the medical room, where a Czech Republic beauty had her legs in stirrups. She was examined by a white-coated customer using an array of medical tools.

The next was the asphyxiation room. One man hand-choked a gorgeous Asian girl, while a brunette Turk's head was bagged in plastic. The slaves weren't even penetrated, meaning the men did it for violent entertainment only.

They viewed the romance room, which was occupied by two women. Since most male customers didn't go there for sensuality, it was used by the rare female customers. Haley watched as two raven-haired, curvy women made love on a bed of roses.

Entering the lavish Champagne room, Manuel was immediately impressed by mirrored ceilings, gold-plated walls, bottles of bubbly, and lines of cocaine. Haley had an eerie feeling from the room, though couldn't figure out why.

"Nice, though not for this situation," Manuel said.

Next, they arrived at the bondage-torture room. Manuel paused in impressiveness. Inside, there were vinyl masks, and whips of all makes and models. Leather, rope, and nylon were at his disposal. There were also other weapons, such as paddles, spiked poles, mid-evil flails, and machetes. Clearly, the cleaning crew never favored that place.

"I like it rough...though it's a little excessive for me," he said, making the girls exhale in relief. He grabbed a small whip, asking, "Can I borrow this?"

"You sir, may keep it."

"And cuffs...can I get a pair for each girl?"

"I'll have them brought to you. Have you decided on a room?"

"I really just want a place I can line them up, use them like fuck toys."

"Ah," the attendant said. "I know the perfect room."

He led them to the orgy room. There, a ten-foot long bed filled the room. A smile came to Manuel's face. "Perfección," he declared.

"As you know, we always leave one guard on duty. Just for your protection," the attendant said.

"I understand."

"I'll do it," Tommy said.

"Very well," the attendant confirmed. As he exited the room, the chained cuffs were brought in.

Tommy stood near the door, keeping a quiet presence.

The slaves were marched inside. All thirteen were lined on the mattress, bent over the edge. It was a tight fit, as they brushed against each other's skin. Manuel tested the whip against his hand, satisfied with the sting.

"Chain one ankle to the other!" he ordered.

Although some didn't understand, they learned from the others. Returning to position, each girl had one ankle chained to the next.

Starting at the end, he whipped a Hispanic slave's curved cheeks. She remained quiet. Unsatisfied, Manuel flogged her again. A slight moan sounded from her, though nothing earth shattering.

Mr. Correa continued to whip, progressively increasing his strength. The pregnant slave's legs began to shake, moaning louder. Even though her skin was tan, the red marks were present across her ass. After his hardest lashing yet, the slave broke into tears.

Satisfaction filled Manuel's face, feeling a surge of testosterone. He continued down the line, unwilling to stop until he saw provable tears. Reaching the last three, he arrived at Haley, Syd and Char. Ms. White's pale skin was more genetically sensitive than most.

Bright red lines stained her thick bottom, as she tapped into the pain, forcing herself to cry. There wasn't any sense in hanging on. Charlotte disagreed, holding out for twenty minutes. A silent, but present tear spilled down her cheek, making Manuel feel manlier than ever.

After whipping Sydney, he had the slaves reverse the line direction. Reclined onto their backs, they were sprawled upon the mattress, chained ankles lifted in a stirrup style. Each leg was interlocked, spread and easily accessible.

Manuel Correa removed his clothes. The 38 year-old man had olive skin and was in prime shape. His arms were strong, stomach ripped. Of course, his most impressive feature was his ten-inch cock.

A connoisseur of fine wines, he knelt down to the ultra blond Sydney. Even before her pregnancy, she had wide hips, a juicy ass, and thick breasts. They only increased with gestation.

Manuel spread her slit with his thumbs, gliding his tongue inside her velvet veil. His wetness mopped her sweet hole, lapping her seeping juices. Getting a mouthful of vulva, his lips tightened in a frantic sucking motion. It was essentially CPR of the vagina.

The harder he sucked, the further back the blond Aussie's eyes rolled. Although she'd already become desensitized to sex as a job, the feeling of lust was forced upon her. As Manuel's veteran tongue spun inside, he rubbed her pregnant belly. His hands roved upward to her bulging breasts, massaging her swollen mammaries.

Her nipples swelled in sensuality, emulating her folds. As his mouth widened, her entire vagina disappeared into his watering orifice. The puffed clitoris vanished while he inhaled like a gust in spring. Her entire sex baked in his hot breath as her wine mulled in his throat.

She broke, as cries of lust echoed into the air. Her legs wanted to constrict upon his head, though were limited by cuffs. The tensed position forced her to work even harder, releasing even more juices.

Having his fill of Sydney, Manuel withdrew his dripping face. After glimpsing Charlotte's dirty blond hair, he craved a new taste. Her defiance left him hungering for challenge, as he attacked.

The dirty blond Canadian swore, *He won't break me this time.*

Her stubbornness made him more determined to break her. He pried her folds with both hands, stretching her beyond anything she had ever experienced. She gasped at the man's aggressiveness. His demeanor made her question her fortitude.

Extending his tongue outward, he rolled it into a wet weapon. Plunging inside her feminine flaps, he pierced her hole in one shot. Feeling his rough entrance, she shook with shock. His goal wasn't to tame her, but conquer her.

His grip upon her lips became greater, as he stretched her even wider. The thrusting tongue plunged, delivering a merciless mouth fucking. The harder he landed, the deeper he dove.

Charlotte shut her eyes, taking slow breaths. *He won't break you,* the stubborn girl assured herself. She was in control, until he added another element. Aligning his nose with her clit, he began tapping it with each thrust. His rounded nose-tip slapped away, pecking like a hungry chicken. He penetrated her so deep, a smacking sound echoed through the room.

His breath began to syphon her juices to the surface. Charlotte's syrup was tapped like a mature maple tree, drained by Manuel's strong tongue. The Canadian slave's body began to tremble. It seemed the harder she fought, the more lust her body produced. With one last drive inside her, the dirty blond lost her oral battle.

Her pregnant belly reached into the air, arching her back. Char's locked legs pulled at her sister-slaves, straining their shared grip. Having self-denied orgasm since she'd arrived, a burning intensity flowed like never before.

Back in Toronto, she was a dominatrix, always maintaining control. Forced from her comfort zone, shame fueled the inner-fire. A once stubborn girl was forced to face captive reality.

Satisfied with his victory, Manuel withdrew. Charlotte's body continued to convulse in humiliation, watching her juices drip down her assailant's cheeks. The thirsty customer turned his gaze toward redheaded Haley. *I've never tasted a redhead before!* He thought, rushing towards her.

The submissive look in her eyes calmed his temperament. Instead of lunging at her, he gently spread her pink slit. It was so delicate and perfect, he almost didn't want to defile it. Almost, but not quite.

He lowered his sticky face to Haley's vagina, striking her floral orchid with his used tongue. She received a fresh dose of friendly fluid, blending the girls' juices in a sensual smoothie of seduction.

His taste buds came alive upon contact. Evidence of her arousal was present in a pearly white haze lining her lips.

Engulfed in her candied crotch, he made love with his mouth. Drops of liquefied sugar spilled into his stomach, defining her tempting taste. Locked in a vaginal French kiss, his face was awash in heavy cream.

Manuel was so enthralled with her flavor he slid downward. Following a faint trail across her taint, he entered her secret garden. Soaking her bronzed-eye, he rimmed the corn with butter.

His round strokes oozed passion, tickling the rim of her sphincter. Pushing inward, he penetrated her pomegranate. Being no veteran, the curvy redhead's sexual senses were thriving. In fact, they only increased with pregnancy. Her vaginal sweetness dripped downward, glazing her savory star with sweetness.

Haley's anal ring tightened around the tongue, as Manuel's penetration went deeper. Feeling the maddening tickle trickle her canal, she followed her new sisters, orgasming in ecstasy.

With every convulsion, her life-filled belly swayed with her full breasts. Like the other girls, her legs tensed, held in place by the adjacent sisters. Manuel continued until Haley went limp with exhaustion.

Upon removal, his face was covered in cream. The next slave would soon be introduced to it. The chain continued along all 13, each of them forced into oral orgasm. When he reached the last, Haley hoped it was over. Though it was only the appetizer for the main course.

Manuel thrust his massive cock inside the last Hispanic slave. He began pumping her deep and fast. Without cumming, he withdrew, sliding directly into the next. Continuing down the line, he arrived at Haley. To her surprise, he skipped her.

Why did he do that? She wondered.

Instead, he went to Sydney, then Charlotte. Haley watched him slam her sister-slaves, forcing them to take every vaginal inch. Just like before, his aroused passion forced orgasms from all.

Withdrawing, he approached Haley. His cock was throbbing with lust, swollen and slick with the juices of 12 others. He ached, as hot cum simmered inside. It had to end up somewhere, and Ms. White was the recipient.

Moving towards Haley, he gripped her thighs, rubbing his lubed cock against her captive carpet. Burying his rod inside her box, her fluid-filled snatch leaked with pleasure. Feeling her sister-slave's juices mix with hers, made her drip even more.

Manuel's spear impaled her tender target, unleashing a sea of endorphins inside her body. The pressure was so intense...yet pleasurable. The man's thick cock felt like a small arm inside her, awakening every nerve and gland.

Reaching his cock's base, an eruption neared. Quickly withdrawing, he slid his mushroom head down to her anus. Haley gasped, feeling the anal invader force its way inside. She completely let go, allowing him full access.

Although more gently, he seized control of the tight territory. Driving deeper inside, he saw her flushed face match the flowing red hair. Her breasts bubbled, pushing her nipples to towering heights.

Once her anus accepted its guest, a fast and furious pounding began. Using her thighs to steady himself, they imprinted her pale skin. Haley's moans filled the air. The more Ms. White's orgasm built up, the more her hole began to restrict. Having held out over two hours and 13 women, Manuel finally broke down. He exploded inside Haley's tight backend.

Feeling the softness spray her colon, Haley lost it too. Her second orgasm was more intense than the first, pushed to a whole other level. Manuel kept cumming, forcing a back-flow to seep out.

As he withdrew, a river seeped outward. The anus slowly closed to its coveted tightness. The man who'd bedded over 10,000 women had never been so satisfied. Looking her in the eye, he said, "I'll be back again. Though next time, there's only one I want."

CHAPTER TWELVE

Darkness filled the guard quarters of *Paraíso,* as Bruce let shower-water cascade his hard body. A dim light barely illuminated the tiled bathroom, a fact he counted on. He hadn't showered in a week, unable to remove his mask or show his face. The moment he entered the brothel doors, his days were numbered. Though none of that mattered. Only Haley's fate was on his mind.

After Ms. White was carried away, the head guard confronted the masked man. Luckily for him, he'd heard enough Spanish over the years. Since Tommy entered with him, the head guard spoke English to them.

"Welcome back, sir," the guard said to Tommy. "Was the man I provided...acceptable to Mr. Cruz?"

"He's as useless as the rest of them," Tommy said in annoyance. "How's the boss, these days?"

"He'll be arriving soon. In the meantime, I'm running the show. The new slave...redhead...I want her put to good use. She's to earn immediately."

"Yes, sir." He turned toward the masked Bruce, "Ve a tu cuarto."

"Sí," Mr. Knight said, understanding the translation of *room*. Assuming that meant guard quarters, he headed towards a separate wing of the building. Although it had been a while, he was once a dedicated customer to the place. Having seen the guards enter, its location was no secret to him.

Entering a large room, the bunks were mostly full. There were about 100-armed guards in the entire complex. Tasked with policing 1000 girls, their weapons evened things out.

As Bruce arrived at the last bed, he saw an unoccupied bunk. It obviously belonged to the man he killed. After settling in, he basked in silence, realizing the guards weren't a chatty bunch. It worked to his advantage.

Each day dragged on as Bruce desperately tried to find Haley. Though, he was constantly put to work, made to guard a different area each night. Haley wasn't in any of them.

He'd overheard the guards talking about the pregnant wing, at least, what he could translate. *She's in there! I have to see her...make sure she's safe,* he thought. The only problem was having the freedom to do so.

Turning off the shower water, he dried his sculpted body with a cheap towel. He quickly put on the black mask, following with the uniform. Sneaking through the building, he avoided the heaviest guard presence, crossing paths of the lowest ranks. There hadn't been an incident in years, breeding a lax attitude to the overnight patrol.

Knight made his way to the pregnant wing. An armed guard blocked the door, asking, "Qué quieres?"

Translating the question, *what do you want,* Bruce thought of an excuse. He answered with the word for *replaced.* "Relevar."

The guard stopped and thought. He knew he wasn't scheduled for replacement, nor did he care. "Sí," he said, handing his machine gun to Bruce, walking away.

Holding the power in his hands, Bruce wondered, *I could get Haley and cut a path for the door.* Though, he knew it would end the same as last time. *I can cover our front, though not our back.*

Brushing off the thought, he entered the pregnant wing. The light was low, as a few girls scattered back into bed. They were chatting, using the lack of guard presence to retain some humanity.

The masked Bruce walked along the bunk beds. The faint glow warmed the girls' faces. Each one pretended to be asleep. They didn't know it, though the guard didn't give a damn. Instead, he studied each one, desperately searching for Haley.

All the girls had dark hair, except for two blondes. *Where the hell is she?* He wondered, coming to the last and empty bed. *If she's dead, I'll...*

A gasp suddenly startled him. Exiting the bathroom, the glow reflected her red hair into his eyes. His search was over. He'd found Haley, and she was safe.

"You!" she said, drawing the attention of the other girls.

Sydney whispered, "Haley! Don't talk to them!"

Charlotte wasn't as politically correct. "Are you fucking nuts? They'll beat you!"

Bruce froze in shock, not knowing what to do. *If I reveal myself in here, one of the slaves could tell. I can't say anything.*

He shook his head in a negative manner, as she zoned in on his eyes. She touched his hand, feeling the same shock that once revived her. *She felt Bruce.* "This man is kind...he's good. He saved my life." She directed her words at him, reaching for his mask. "Your eyes...they're like...someone I once knew." He pulled away, as she started to tear up.

Sydney and Charlotte got out of bed, leading Haley away. "Excuse her," Sydney said, trying to defuse the situation. "Those pregnant hormones drive us batty."

Charlotte pointed to her head, saying, "Crazy...loco." The two girls hurried Haley back into bed.

Bruce continued to stand there, lost within the angelic afterglow. His heart broke, yet was soothed at the same time. He slowly backed away, heading for the door. Upon exiting, he was more confused than ever. Knight felt cruel giving Haley empty hope.

Though the risky act wasn't in vain. Not only did he know where she was, but he found her allies too. In order to turn things around, he'd need every person he could trust. They watched her back, therefore they'd keep his secret.

*****

Thursday arrived, as the night guards did their usual thing. The head guard always helped himself to the women, allowing his men the same privilege. Like the previous Thursday, the 13 pregnant slaves lined the showroom.

Bruce's heart thumped with opportunity. *This is my shot! I can be alone with her!* Haley locked onto his gaze, recognizing the compassionate guard's eyes. She hoped he'd choose her. He looked around, scoping his competition. It was first come, first serve. There were 12 men, granting one a ménage. Though, Bruce only had eyes for the redhead.

"I choose first," the head guard said. He walked down the line, passing Haley. Bruce quietly exhaled, until the man stopped. Backtracking, he took her by the hand. "I choose the red hair. Now, go fuck."

A look of disappointment filled both their faces. The men immediately went for their favorite choice. Having only two more options, Mr. Knight lunged toward Sydney and Charlotte. He knocked over three men to get them, grabbing both their hands.

"Someone's horny," Sydney proclaimed.

"Gonna be a long night," Charlotte added.

*****

The three entered an empty room, getting their turn to perform. Bruce was uneasy, starting to question his options. *What if they're not really her friends? In a place like this, survival is all that matters. They may turn us both in.*

"Relax," Sydney said in a warm voice, placing a hand on him. "No need to be nervous."

"That's unusual. They usually won't shut up...even if we don't know what they're saying," Charlotte said, adding a hand to Knight's shoulder. They pushed him down upon the bed. The Canadian reached for his mask, as he quickly stopped her.

"No!" he shouted, blocking her hand.

"If it means *that* much to you, keep it," Char said, leaving it.

"No need to be shy with us," Sydney said, as the guard remained silent. "OK, we'll start elsewhere." She removed his boots.

Charlotte unbuckled Bruce's pants, pulling everything off. He remained stiff and uncomfortable, sending silent signals of displeasure. Both parties had conflicting goals, as the girls had a job to do; he had an identity to protect.

They continued undressing him, forcing his thick, 9-inches to drop out. Charlotte's eyebrows raised in surprise, not expecting such a package. Sydney removed Bruce's shirt, leaving him masked and naked. "This might be the first time...the client is less interested than we are," the blond Aussie said.

A wicked smirk came across Char's face. "Then maybe...I'll actually enjoy this. I guess it *is* a night of firsts."

Bruce silently thought to himself, *I have to stop them...without revealing my identity! It's impossible. I'll just have to fight the pleasure. I won't enjoy anything until she's safe. I won't be pleased, while Haley's forced to screw scum.*

His thoughts were interrupted by feminine hands shoving him flat. The nude pregnant beauties crawled over him, Charlotte being the most aggressive. Bruce tried to stop them with a simple, "No!"

However, he was quickly quieted by Char squatting upon his mask. For the first time in a while, she'd regained control, forcing someone else to please her. It freed her dominant personality. Holding the baby-weight with her knees, she spread her moist slit, claiming her favorite position: on top.

In order to breathe, Bruce's tongue protruded the mask's mouth slot. His nostrils inhaled a maternal aroma. Having no choice but to comply, his red dart stretched into the creamy crease.

Feeling it penetrate her hole, Charlotte gasped. "It appears this one's found other uses for a tongue," she said sarcastically.

Bruce's lengthy appendage stretched beyond its limits, exploring her sweet roll. Cinnamon tones sparked his senses, as he climbed her cave walls like an expert spelunker. His one goal was to get her off, withholding his own pleasure. He refused to betray Haley with orgasm.

The more Charlotte squatted, the farther his tongue was forced inside. Bruce's head was fully engulfed. With every stroke, smooth sensations brushed his tongue. It was like licking vanilla soft serve.

A new sensation challenged his mission of ejaculatory denial. Sydney widened her mouth, slowly swallowing his rod. As she reached his base, he jittered, feeling his cock-head lodged into her throat.

She primed his pump with a few deep bobs. Disengaging from the pole of power, she squatted over his cock. The blond Aussie plugged the electric head into her vaginal socket. Slowly sinking downward, her creamy canal enveloped the manly column. Already slick with saliva, she slid down to the base. It penetrated so deeply, her fetus kicked back in defense. The two girls faced each other, watching mutual pleasure.

Charlotte's eyes rolled in lust as the sound of slurping filled the air. Bruce was forced to drink so furiously; he emptied her quicker than she could produce. Her hanging folds were sucked into his mouth, as she rested her hands upon Bruce's hard chest. Finding another set planted there, she overlapped her sister-slave's soft fingers.

Sydney carefully bobbed upon Knight's commanding cock. The girls locked eyes, watching their pregnant bellies and breasts sway in gentle rhythm. They held hands, sliding up each other's arms. Reaching outward, they traced their breast bubbles, riding the roller coaster of curves down full-hips and ass.

Sliding over to the smooth pubis, they headed up the gestational mountain. Both of them had brightly painted fingernails of deep red, glowing in the mood-setting lights. The long acrylics traced the protruding bellies, leaving a set of chills in their wake.

The magic touches stopped at their rounded aureoles. They massaged each other gently, though Charlotte's hold was more aggressive. Sydney's hips gyrated upon Bruce's cock, torturing his stubborn pole with wet lust. Her g-spot swelled in time with Knight's ever-hardening manhood.

Syd's intensity grew, as Char moved to the Aussie's thick nipples. An aggressive milking motion began. The Canadian's fingers pinched the aureole base, using her wrists to perform a sensual rhythm.

Gasping deeply, Sydney felt an immediate spark between Bruce's impaling and her molested mammaries. Charlotte's vaginal wine continued to spill. His sucking was so intense her juices flowed at an abnormally aggressive rate.

Deciding to return the favor, the blond Aussie began milking Charlotte. Her technique was different, more of a caress than a tug. They gazed at each other, watching breasts swell, feeling glands fill.

Sydney leaned inward, prompting Charlotte to meet her halfway. Their tongues reached for each other, creating a triangle of passion. With Bruce's American citizenship, it was truly an international event. In one hour, they'd accomplished more than the United Nations ever had. That's not saying much.

The three continued the pleasure-cycle. Their flow was so in-sync, when one broke the other followed. Sydney disengaged from the kiss, feeling a sexual eruption rumble her core.

A loud moan filled the air, as Syd's thick thighs clamped upon Bruce's cock. An array of fireworks popped through her body, tingling head to toe. Charlotte's milking grip reached maximum intensity, forcing Sydney to lactate for the first time ever.

Streams of relief sailed from the Aussie's ducts, squirting white rain upon Bruce and Charlotte. The dirty-blond Canadian bathed in warm liquid, feeling Mr. Knight's tongue plunge her.

Char was the next one to break, clamping her thighs upon the masked man's head. Syd's gentle milking forced a river from Char's big breasts, spraying onto Sydney and Bruce's bellies.

As drops of lovely lactation covered Mr. Knight, he was losing the lustful battle. Gripping onto Charlotte's hips, he pulled upward, forcing her off. Surprised by the act, Syd dismounted as well. Bruce gripped his cock tightly, replacing pleasure with pain. Within moments, his urge diminished. "I'm sorry...it's not you...it's me."

"He speaks English!" Sydney accused.

Oh shit, Bruce silently thought. "Uh...little," he covered.

"Man, I grew up just across the U.S. border. That accent's not fooling anyone," Charlotte said. "Who *are* you?"

Bruce exhaled, almost thankful for the forced error. "What matters to you...is who I'm not. I'm no guard. Consider me an ally."

"So, do you wear ski masks for fun...or fashion?" Charlotte sarcastically asked.

"Survival. Let's just say...I'm an outlaw...hunted by Victor Cruz."

Sydney cut in. "Forgive me...but back home...we'd call you a drongo. Why would you come to the one place he'd find you?"

He removed his mask, pushing away all worries. "Because there's a life more important than mine. She's someone I'd sacrifice my own life to save."

The Aussie studied the man's appearance. "I know you...your face. Wait! You're the man from the island. Haley's man! Your name is...Bruce! You're alive!"

Charlotte cut in. "At least I don't feel so...ineffective anymore. I was beginning to think I'd lost my touch."

"As I said...it's not you. I won't betray her love...with sex or anything else."

Syd gripped her heart, "I'm such a sucker for romance."

"Romance is foreign to a place like this. Death is not. It's no place for human beings."

Sydney studied him harder. "Your eyes...last night! That was you in our room."

"It was. I had to see Haley...make sure she was OK."

Charlotte looked shocked. "And I just thought she was nuts. At least we know she has good taste."

A fan of love stories, tears filled Sydney's eyes. "She swore you'd come to free her...keep your promise. I guess good men really do exist...you saved her."

"I haven't done anything until we're free."

"Well...you just got two more passengers," Charlotte proclaimed. "We're coming along for the ride."

"I'll need every able-bodied person I can find...can trust. We're outgunned, though not outnumbered. It's up to you both...spread the word to any girl who wants out."

"Everyone wants out of this whorehouse," Charlotte quipped. "The question is...how many of them can understand us?"

Bruce held up a single finger. "Tell them one word. *Libertad.*"

"What's that?" Sydney asked.

"*Freedom,*" Bruce said with conviction.

Sydney smiled. "Haley will be thrilled to hear you're alive!"

"No. Don't tell her. If I die in the process...I don't want her to grieve again...mourn me twice. Wait until this all shakes out...I'll tell her myself."

Charlotte cut in. "I hate to be a buzz kill here, but a plan would be nice, eh?"

"I'm working on it. Though no matter what we do, many will die. If it's too risky, I'll understand if you back out."

"No way in hell," they both shouted.

"Good. Spread the word...but remember...only those you trust. One way or the other...an uprising is coming."

*****

Bruce took his current shift, guarding the theme-room hallway. He'd waited a few days, closely studying the shift-changes of each guard. There was a short window of time he could search each place.

Arriving in the theme-rooms, he had to act quickly. He tore through each one, searching for things to weaponize. At first, he considered the guard armory, though it was off the brothel ground, denying slaves any access.

Each theme-room offered small possibilities, but nothing large enough to sustain an offensive. The medical room had some tools, while the asphyxiation room had rope. *It's just not enough!* He thought, about to give up. That's when he entered the torture room. His eyes widened like a sadistic porn lover in the 1970's.

First there was the multitude of whips. Though it was the spiked-poles, mid-evil flails, and machetes that caught his attention.

He picked up a steel club topped with a razor sharp spike. "Play ball," he said.

He knew time was running out, as he returned the club to the wall. Hurrying out, he knew there was one last room. Planning to avoid it, the place was too painful to enter. However, he knew it could be the last chance to pay final respects.

Bruce quietly entered the Champagne room. *They didn't change a damn thing,* he thought in disbelief. It was a bittersweet fact, knowing it would only conjure more memories of the night Carolina was killed.

He turned on the golden light, watching the room light up like a kingly tomb. Bruce lay on the bed, staring up at mirrored ceilings. Carolina's fire red hair shined back in his eyes. Her curved hips stretched across the room. The words she spoke echoed in his ears. '*I'm pregnant.'*

His eyes shut, as he remembered the tightness of her anal grip. Each moment offered a lifetime of pleasure…a life that was denied them both.

A voice suddenly startled him. "What the hell are you doing in here?" Tommy Johns yelled. Having heard unusual noises for that time of night, he checked it out.

The masked Bruce rose, standing at attention. He lowered his voice, using a heavily accented tone. "No comprende?"

"Do you understand this?" Tommy yelled, striking Bruce's masked face.

Holding steady, Knight kept his composure. Tommy studied Bruce's eyes, getting a sudden flash of his old nemesis.

Luckily for Bruce, the guards were given protection of identity. No one could remove or order their masks removed. Since some of the abducted girls were family members and neighbors, it would bring shame upon their families.

Knowing his identity was safe, Bruce tilted his head downward, avoiding further eye-contact.

"You're the one from the island...the plane," Tommy suddenly realized. "There was something strange about you then...something stranger now. Well, you like this room so much...you can guard it permanently. You'll stay in this room...until permitted to exit."

Bruce nodded, indicating he understood.

Tommy backed away, keeping his eyes on Bruce. As he exited the room, Knight exhaled. However, his problems were far from gone. *How will I tell the girls my plan? I counted on guarding their quarters.*

Taking another look around, he realized something even more daunting awaited him. He'd have to spend the night with old ghosts.

*****

Sydney and Charlotte stared at each other, as Haley's soft cries rose to the top bunks. She'd cried every night, trying not to let them hear. They once felt pity for her pain, though now they felt blame.

Sydney whispered to Charlotte. "We should tell her!"

"Too unstable!" Char replied.

"I have to...try," Syd said, moving down to Haley's bunk. "Mate...it's gonna be OK. I promise." She hugged her.

"I didn't mean for you to hear. I just miss him."

"Bruce?" Sydney exhaled, trying to stay strong. "You'll see him again...I can feel it."

"No, I won't. I've resorted to chasing guards...thinking they're him. I've lost my mind."

"What if I told you...we're planning an escape?"

"It wouldn't bring him back."

"No...though, it'll free you to look for him. Listen, you told me...he promised to come for you. Have you lost your faith in him?"

"I'll always believe in Bruce."

"Then dry your tears. Wherever you are...he'll find you. But now...find hope in the fact...we're getting the hell out of here."

Haley wiped her wet face, as Charlotte dropped down from her bunk. "It's time to spread the word. We found a bilingual bisexual. The bisexual part doesn't really apply here, just had a nice ring to it."

"How will we do it?" Haley asked.

"We're still working on that," Charlotte said cryptically. "Though...there's one absolute."

"What?" Haley asked.

"We must tell the girls in here. They'll tell the girls in other wings...be ready to fight for their lives...and their *libertad*. Fight for their freedom."

CHAPTER THIRTEEN

Guards lined *Paraíso's* private runway. Victor Cruz stepped off the plane, happy to be back home. Tommy approached him. "Mr. Cruz, it's good to see you, sir."

"Has the redhead behaved?"

"She's submitted to her new role rather nicely. A good earner, drawn major interest from the clientele."

"Then I suppose she'll live a while longer. At least, until her worth runs out."

"Yes, sir. The staff's prepared your room and meal."

"I'm not hungry or tired. In fact, I want to see the books...make sure there's no selective accounting going on. My *papa* once had an accountant *fired*...literally. The guards set him ablaze."

"I would've liked to have seen that, sir."

"Fail me...and you will."

*****

The pregnant slaves were lined up in the showroom, awaiting their next client. Spanning Haley's few weeks, she served multiple men a day. She faked pleasure, though cried during most. Luckily for her, many of them got off on misery.

Mr. Manuel Correa made his usual visit. Decked out in another Versace suit, he carefully walked the slave line. He studied each girl carefully, though in reality, his decision was made after his last session.

"Would you like to use them all again, sir?" the attendant asked.

"No," he said, stopping at Haley. "The redhead...alone."

Haley gasped, seeing a deviant look in his eye. *God help me if he chooses the torture room.*

"Excellent choice, sir. Would you like a theme room?"

"I'm in the mood for some fine...Champagne."

"Very well, sir. Follow me."

Haley calmed a bit, happy to hear it wasn't the bondage area. Sydney rubbed Ms. White's back, offering luck as she always did. With the word spread, the slaves awaited Bruce's signal. They just didn't know what it was.

*****

Manuel led Haley into the Champagne room. Upon entering, a gasp sounded from behind them. They quickly turned, surprised at the masked guard's presence. Though, *he* was the one truly shocked. It was Bruce.

He locked upon Haley's eyes, as she returned the gaze. A pleasant smile crossed her face. For some odd reason, he made her feel safe.

"You know this man?" Manuel asked, noticing the joy.

"I've seen him around," she said cryptically.

Manuel pulled her head away, turning it towards him. *"They pay him to guard...I pay to fuck.* Forget he's even here. Tonight, you belong to me!"

"Of course," Haley said, sliding her hand into his pants. She squeezed his large cock, stroking it. The massive member grew inside her hand.

"That's more like it," he said, removing his clothes.

Bruce watched in disbelief. He silently thought, *Whatever happens, I must not interfere. It'll screw everything up. I either detach from the moment...or get us both killed!* Following his advice, he shut his eyes.

Mr. Correa lifted the pregnant girl into his arms, laying her on the plush bed. Before joining her, he headed towards a side-table. It featured a bottle of fine Champagne. A few long strands of cocaine rested on a glass surface. It was a strong blend, straight from a narco's kitchen.

He picked up the coke, bringing a tiny straw to his nostril. Snorting the line in record time, he grabbed his nose afterward, not used to the strength. A new energy filled him, as he brought the glass surface to Haley.

"No," she insisted. "The baby." She placed her hand on her stomach.

Bruce's eyes darted open. *If he forces her to snort, I'll break his neck before the straw hits her nostril.*

Manuel nodded, placing it down. He turned toward the Champagne. Knowing Cocaine was an aggressive stimulant, worry filled Haley. *Will it make him violent?* She wondered.

Seeing the drug removed, Bruce chastised himself, *My anger must be kept under control! No matter what happens...I can't cause a scene!* He shut his eyes again.

Climbing on the mattress, Manuel held the bottle over Haley's stomach. He popped the cork, firing it into the ceiling. An ocean of bubbly rained over Haley's body. She gasped.

"Relax," Manuel said, kneeling down to her vaginal smile. He continued pouring the cold liquid onto the peak of her belly, letting it cascade like a carbonated waterfall.

Haley tried to stay still, as the alcohol spilled in both directions. One stream slid toward her breasts, pooling in the valley of cleavage. The other wave went downward, trickling through her vagina.

Manuel positioned his open mouth at her clitoris. The engorged button acted as a slide, redirecting the liquid onto his tongue. He continued to lap away, as a mattress puddle formed.

After a few moments, he stopped pouring. Instead, he dug his wet dagger into her sweet spot, slowly following the upward trail. Licking the globe of pregnancy, he landed at her breasts. Sucking the pool between the cleavage, he poured more liquid on her erect nipples, stiffening them more.

Engulfing each red tip with his mouth, he sucked every drop. Licking back down to her vagina, he spread her with his fingers. Inserting the bottleneck, he filled her human flume with liquor.

Haley gasped at the growing pressure inside her. The cold merged with the popping fizz bubbles, stimulating her sensitive silk. Bruce managed to keep his eyes closed, fighting the urge to check on her.

After waiting a few moments, Manuel spread her wide. Placing his mouth lips to vaginal ones, he began drinking. Feeling Manuel's hand press down on her outer pubic area, she had no choice but to let go, expelling the Champagne into his mouth.

He drank the combined juices, noticing an added sweetness. Feeling the air-sucked champagne exit her, she was further stimulated. Right before it emptied, a small orgasm crossed her body. It gently vibrated throughout.

Right as Manuel finished, he quickly headed towards Haley's mouth. His cheeks were pouched, indicating he'd saved some for her. Approaching her lips, he pulled them open.

"No! We don't kiss clients!" she emphasized.

Ignoring her warning, Manuel engulfed her lips, releasing the concoction into her mouth. She was forced to swallow it, feeling his tongue swirl inside her. Although the on-duty guard would've stopped such a thing, Bruce could not. It would draw too much attention for a minor offense.

Removing the kiss, Mr. Correa looked her in the eyes. His pupils were wider than before, as beads of sweat poured down his skin. His body jittered, cock twitched. The look on his face resembled a pride of lions eyeing a dove.

Manuel quickly rolled off her, retrieving the cocaine-lined glass. He brought it with him, rejoining Haley on the bed. Blowing one of the lines onto the slave's curvy stomach, one more remained.

He took the straw in his hands. His ultra aroused cock was placed at her dripping hole. Wasting no time with ease, the anxious man thrust inside. Haley moaned, feeling him bang her in long, hard strokes. With every landing, the white powder danced upon her belly. It continued for a while, until he leaned in for refreshment. Using the straw, he snorted the cocaine-line off her skin.

A rush of air sailed from his nose, as he pinched his nostrils again. A burning sensation set his brain ablaze. "Woo!" he screamed, getting a crazed look in his eyes. The banging continued, harder and faster.

Bruce's eyes opened again. His heart rate began to speed, nearly matching the drugged customer. Danger was in the air and he sensed it. He knew he had to restrain himself; he just didn't know if he could.

Haley's moans filled the air, as she'd never been fucked so furiously. He gripped her throat, beginning to squeeze. Bruce Knight's fists crumbled into a ball, feeling his body reject his brain's command.

Mr. Correa released his choking grip, grabbing the glass with the cocaine. He forced it to her nose, yelling, "Snort, bitch!"

"No! My baby!" she screamed, turning her head away. He began slapping her face, continuing to drive his cock inside her.

Suddenly, a look of ultimate darkness filled his gaze. Fury possessed Manuel, as he lifted the glass surface, ready to bludgeon her with it.

His hands rose above his head. Suddenly, the weapon crashed down upon himself. Haley screamed, seeing Manuel's head shatter with the glass. Bruce covered her mouth, while tossing the dead customer off the bed.

Haley shook, looking in the masked man's eyes. She slowly reached upward, removing the disguise. Gasping so deeply, her lungs nearly burst. Blood drained from her face, rendered as pale as a friendly ghost. Tears dropped like sleet, as Bruce wiped them away. "Promise kept," he assured her.

"Bruce!" she proclaimed, finally accepting it wasn't a mirage. Embracing him like a sea-bound survivor to ship-wreckage, she refused to let go. The two became inseparable, merging so closely, their hearts synced. "I thought you were dead."

"I am," he said, confusing her.

She paused the embrace. "What?"

"The guard on the island...died there. The man taken from the brothel...is back. Only this time...he's come for blood."

Staring into his strong eyes, Haley was reborn as well. She moved toward his lips. A shared kiss refueled their souls, healing every wound inside. Two broken hearts merged, forming something stronger than before their past selves.

The kiss of passion continued, slowly ingesting every drop of each other. As it ended, they moved to each other's necks, inhaling their natural scents. Breaking his own rule, Bruce tossed caution to the dogs. Whatever happened from *that* moment was a fate he'd accept.

Haley pulled off Knight's shirt, removing his pants even quicker. Ms. White hungered for his touch, needing more than sex. She needed to feel his existence inside her, convincing her body of his life. Having already mourned him, she truly never expected to touch his flesh again. For the moment, they entered an altered-reality, absent of slaves, captivity and floor-bound bodies.

Kneeling down to his thickness, Haley swallowed it. Knight's eyes rolled back, craving her warm, gentle sucking technique. She slowly dipped his rod in saliva, branding it with her mouth.

Growing harder by the moment, he ran his hands through her red hair. Each strand flowed through his fingers like waves of fire. She pressed on his chest, leading him flat on the bed.

Disengaging her mouth from his cock, she climbed on top of him. Replacing one orifice for the other, she squatted upon his swollen spear. The curvy redhead rode Bruce like a stallion. Every muscle bulged on the tense man, as he struggled to withhold flowing desire.

For a moment, his gaze exited hers, focusing on the mirrored ceiling. Mr. Knight realized, he was granted a second chance. It was like reliving his last night with Carolina. However, he wasn't going to let it end the same.

Staring up at the reflection, he remembered the unique perspective it offered. From above, his past and present merged into one. Red hair flew in the air-conditioned breeze, dancing in an unnatural wind. A feminine hourglass redefined itself with each movement. Some curves were added, while others were absorbed within. Her luscious crescent hips were enhanced in the reflection, stretching into infinity.

Though, he knew he could never go back. He no longer wanted to. Haley was now number one in his heart. He tilted his gaze away from the mirror, focusing on his lover's eyes. She was truly one of a kind.

Haley rode him as her pregnant belly swayed. She placed her hands on his chest, using his washboard stomach to propel her baby-weight upon his pole. Gravity helped her back down.

Bruce reached out for her, rubbing his hands upon their encapsulated creation. He felt the baby move, almost reaching out for their protection. It was a feeling he never thought he'd experience. *This won't end like the last time. I won't let them die, even if I have to sacrifice myself.*

His stroking her stomach was the most sexual act she'd ever *performed*. He reached her nipples, massaging the swollen mammaries. Returning the favor, she squeezed his too, making them rise to their tender limits. Her red nails traced his pectoral muscles, rising up his neck, encircling his lips.

Knight swallowed her finger, sucking on the soft skin. She let it sink into his throat, while riding him with growing intensity. Removing his hands from her breasts, he held her thick hips, thrusting her higher and faster upon his rod. His teeth gnawed her finger, as the dual sensations caused her to break.

Bruce's bulbous cock struck her inflamed g-spot. Haley shuttered in the golden light. Her body arched, face tensed, retaining class and beauty. She had the grace of a queen, or of an angel.

As her hole constricted in lust, Bruce spilled his seed. Weeks of denied desire flowed through her body, enriching Haley with everlasting love. As they finished, she leaned in, placing her warm cheek upon his chest.

Bruce remained focused, knowing it was no time to rest. Their moment of fantasy was over. Eternal reality was about to begin.

Haley said, "From this moment on...if we die, I'm ready."

"Many will die...but not you. I came here to free you...that's what I'll do. Even if it costs me my own life."

"Without you...I have no life. Besides, when they discover Mr. Correa's body, they'll kill us both anyway."

"By the time they realize he's missing...he'll be the least of their problems. We'll either be free...or dead. Either way...we'll take the fuckers with us."

"We don't have a prayer against their weapons. We can't do this alone."

"We're not alone."

"Who else do we have?"

"The two blond slaves...your friends."

"Charlotte and Sydney?"

"They know. They're on board. If their word's been kept...the others have been told as well."

She sat up, "You mean...*you're* the one they're waiting for? They didn't even tell me!"

"I chose them from the lineup."

"You...had sex with them?"

"I didn't cum...if that's what you're asking."

"Really? Pretty impressive...*I* couldn't even hold out. In the shower...never mind."

"Anyway, I asked them not to tell you. I couldn't give you hope...when that hope may never have arrived."

"Don't you understand, Bruce? You coming here...keeping your promise...that's all the hope I ever needed. It's enough."

"Then hang on to it. Come tomorrow, we're gonna need all the hope we can get."

She turned her head, seeing a pool of blood on the carpet. "Where do we hide his body?"

Bruce got up, dragging Manuel under the bed. He pulled a Persian carpet over the rug stain. "Done."

"What now?"

"Go back to the girls...tell them to await my signal."

"What signal?"

"An alarm. Then gunfire...lots of it. Tell every slave to make a run for the torture room."

"The place with the disturbing things on the wall?"

"Come tomorrow night...they'll be the most beautiful things you've ever seen. A path will be cleared. You'll grab the deadliest things you can find. Then, we rush the exit doors. Any hesitation to kill...will get you killed. They are to head west...into the woods. Got it?"

"Yeah. Where will *you* be?"

"Leading the charge."

*****

A full day went by as word quietly trickled to every brothel slave. The clock struck 3 A.M.. Bruce Knight approached the exit-door guard with a lighter, silently motioning for a cigarette. His lack of voice wasn't one of translation. It was one of strategy.

The masked guard disengaged his trigger-finger. Reaching into his pockets, he searched for smokes. Bruce pooled a hidden swig of vodka in his mouth, blowing the fueled flame at the guard's eyes. Momentary blindness struck the enemy. Twisting the masked neck in one swift movement, the guard was silenced.

As the enemy fell, Bruce caught the body. One loud noise would ruin everything. He added the guard's machine gun to his own, inheriting a second smoke grenade.

Making his way into the guard-quarter hallway, he stood at the exit. An emergency alarm panel was directly at his side. He balled his fist, taking one last breath. At that moment, he remembered a piece of advice an Army Chaplain once gave. Seeing Bruce struggling with inner demons, the man sat beside him. '*Son, the path to spiritual redemption often passes through fire. The one who faces the flames, emerges whole. The one who fears them, is consumed.*'

A look of determination crossed his face, as he punched the alarm panel with his fist. A blaring alarm was triggered, echoing across the brothel. Knight pulled one smoke grenade's pin, tossing the weapon into the hallway. He knelt down, securing two machine guns into his armpits.

The evacuation began. An array of confused voices filled the air. Tired, masked men evacuated their room, into the hazy hall. They couldn't see, trying to feel their way forward. Bruce stayed at the smoke cloud's edge.

Knight waited, knowing timing was everything. He'd need them to coagulate together, presenting one big target. There were more guards on duty: the outer-perimeter and separate wings. Though, the collective strength would take a hit.

Once the hallway was clogged with guards, the first man emerged from the smoke. He paused in shock, facing Bruce's barrels. Mr. Knight unloaded, filling the man full of lead. Once the first went down, others began to fall. Screams filled the air, though the bullets silenced their cries.

Orange pops of fire tinted Bruce's body, as every muscle was defined. The kick from the guns would've knocked the average man down, though Knight held strong. Sparks spilled out, as he made sure to cross-streams, covering every inch.

The last bullets emptied, as only screams remained. Of the 100-armed guards in *Paraíso,* 50 were silenced. Out of ammunition, Bruce tossed the automatic weapons aside.

He exited the hallway, making his way toward the stairs. The slave exodus began, as the masses ran for the torture room. Exterior guards began to enter the building, forming a defensive line. They began shooting the unarmed slaves.

Knight pulled a handgun from his side, covering their flight. He took out a few spare guards, while their numbers continued to grow. "Faster!" he shouted to the girls. Once his ability to provide cover ended, they would be sitting ducks.

"Bruce!" Haley yelled, running to join him. Charlotte and Sydney grabbed her, stopping the foolish act.

He yelled at her. "Go with them! I'll come...trust me."

She trembled in fear, as tears rimmed her eyes. The girls ferried her up the stairs, towards the weapons.

The guard presence was nearing full-force. Their return fire grew heavier. More girls were shot in the back, spilling down to Bruce's feet. Knight fired a few more shots, continuing to save lives. All the while, he backtracked up the stairs.

Saving his final two bullets as a last resort, he pulled his remaining smoke grenade. Tossing it down to the growing guard-line, he bought himself a minute to gather his force. He ran to the torture room. It was overflowing with slaves, more arriving from different angles. They stripped the walls of every weapon imaginable. Bruce managed to secure two spiked clubs.

He handed one to Haley, checking on Charlotte and Sydney. Char had a whip, Syd had a machete. "You girls know how to handle those?"

"Pretty straight forward," Sydney said, making a hacking motion.

All of a sudden, a whip sailed by Bruce's head, crackling. He turned, seeing an errant guard out cold. Looking back, he saw

Charlotte holding it proudly. "Did I ever mention...I was a dominatrix?" she asked.

"Whatever you just did...do it again soon," Bruce said, turning towards Haley.

"I've never been the killing kind," she said fearfully.

"Nor was I...once. Killers kill for death. Survivors kill for life," he looked up at the growing crowd of slaves. He shouted to the group. "S*urvivors*!"

A cheer sounded, as the word was understood by all.

Holding up his club, he added one last word. "*Libertad*!"

Another cheer sounded, as Bruce led them forward. "Go to the back," he told Haley, who was happy to obey. She dragged Charlotte and Sydney with her.

The group arrived at the stair's upper edge. A thick haze still hung in the air, as all remaining guards formed a defensive line at the bottom. The path to freedom ran through them. Although the slaves vastly outnumbered the men, the automatic arms provided a daunting task to overcome.

Silence reigned, as Victor appeared out front. Tommy followed him, glaring up at the mysterious rebel and his feminine army.

Mr. Cruz addressed the masked stranger. "I don't know your grievance, sir...but I am indeed impressed by your negotiating skills. Enlighten me with your name...your face."

Bruce yanked off his mask, tossing it down to his old boss' feet.

Anger filled Tommy's face, as the responsibility was ultimately his. "Sir, I saw his body in the pit...with the dogs. I swear."

"Shut up!" Victor angrily shouted, losing his usual cool. Cruz returned his attention to Bruce. "I now remember why I spared your life...instead of slaying you. Power. It's why I brought you into my inner circle, embraced you as a brother..."

"You're no brother. Brother's don't murder spouses, force their kin into abducting innocent girls."

"I believe you're mistaken, Mr. Knight. I offered you a choice in the matter. You chose to join me...instead of your dead slave in the dog pit. Therefore, I ask you...is the devil's assistant...any less responsible than the devil himself?"

"And someday...I'll pay for those sins. But today...you're the one to be judged."

"Don't be a fool, Mr. Knight. Give up, and we'll discuss a fair resolution...at least for yourself. You don't really think these whores can defeat my armed men. How do you plan on escaping?"

"By facing the fire." Bruce lifted his spiked club into the air, igniting a cheer. After it quieted, a moment of tense silence sounded. Suddenly, he shouted, "Libertad!"

An angry roar echoed *Paraíso's* walls. Sensing the coming fight, Victor whispered into Tommy's ear. He quickly escaped into a nearby room.

Bruce led the army of estrogen down the stairs. Tommy Johns shouted to the masked guards, "Fire!"

As the slave-line reached the halfway point, deafening gunfire filled the air. Cries sounded as women began tumbling down. Some were shot, others tripped by stilled bodies. Many stopped in fear, therefore halting the line. The still targets froze, watching their friends bleed with bullets. Refocusing on Bruce's advance, his bravery propelled them forward again.

A hail of bullets whizzed past Knight's head, as he dove into the enemy crowd. Knocking a few men down, he began swinging the spiked club. Grabbing hold of a gun, he turned it upon the guards, taking a few out. However, it didn't stop hundreds of slaves from falling to their deaths. The majority continued on anyway.

The first wave of women finally broke through. Hand to hand fighting began, as the guard's ammo neared emptiness. The masked men began swinging their gun-butts, beating the girls down. However, they returned in kind by clawing the guards' eyes.

Bruce returned to swinging his club, bludgeoning multiple enemies at a time. The room began to overflow with people, as the slaves kept coming. As more arrived, less space became available. One barely had room to move, creating a battlefield of suffocation.

Haley, Charlotte, and Sydney approached the maddening mess. Although hundreds of slaves fell, the crush of femininity overwhelmed the guards. Char led the way, hurling her whip at every man she could. A frantic Haley looked around, desperately searching for Bruce.

Mr. Knight fought off three men, smashing their skulls with his spiked club. A fourth approached him from a back blind spot. Haley spotted him. Looking down at her club, instinct took over. Without thought, she pursued the enemy from a similar position of surprise. Charging with all her strength, she impaled the masked man in the back of the head. Bruce turned in shock, face to face with her.

She gasped, wiping the specks of blood from her face. "Stay by my side," he told her. Another guard charged her from behind, swinging his gun-butt at her pregnant stomach. Before he could reach her, Charlotte's whip lashed around the guard's neck. Pulling hard, she held him down with her foot, crushing his windpipe.

Sydney watched, suddenly approached by a dagger-wielding guard. He threatened, "I'll cut that baby from you, whore!"

She suddenly remembered the machete in her hand. A once in a lifetime opportunity filled her head. "You call *that* a knife?" She slowly lifted the machete. "*This*...is a knife." As much as she hated *Crocodile Dundee's* stereotypes, the line was too tempting not to deliver.

Throwing down his pathetic knife, he ran into Charlotte's whip. He was knocked backward into Syd's feet. Angry at his threat to her baby, she swung the machete, splitting his masked face in two.

The sheer number of slaves began taking its toll on the guards. The three girls and Bruce pushed further into the crowd, getting separated in the maddening fight. Some had already reached the exit doors, trying to break the chains.

Thirty hellish minutes flew by, as male and female corpses polluted the showroom floor. Bruce took his spiked club to the door-chains, breaking them. As it opened, fresh air struck their faces. A cheer filled the room, as Mr. Knight looked around. All the guards were down. "We're free!" he yelled.

The cheer continued, as the slaves broke towards freedom. He spotted Charlotte and Sydney, hugging them. "Where's Haley?" he asked.

They both looked at him in shock. "We thought she was with you?" a worried Sydney said.

Bruce frantically checked the female bodies, joined by the girls. There was no sign of her, as a loud sound came from an adjacent room.

"Tommy," Knight said, realizing his mortal enemy wasn't amongst the dead.

He pulled his handgun, rechecking the ammo. There were two bullets left. Continuing towards the room, Charlotte followed behind him. He held his hand up. "Go," he said.

"But Haley!" Syd shouted.

"I must face them alone. I'm the one who kidnapped her...I'm the one who must free her. Head west...opposite the sun, into the woods. We'll find you."

Charlotte said, "Be careful."

A worried look filled Sydney's face. "Bring back our girl."

Bruce nodded, heading toward the room. Charlotte and Sydney exited towards freedom.

*****

Haley tried to call Bruce's name, though Tommy hand-gagged her. Realizing the battle was lost, he followed Victor's backup plan. Inside Mr. Cruz's office, he pulled up a hidden hatch within the marble floor. It made a big bang, alerting Bruce to his whereabouts.

The smell of mold, piss and feces rose from beneath, along with faint light. "Go...or you and your baby die!" Tommy threatened.

Tears spilled from Haley's eyes, as she was forced to squeeze her pregnant form into the dark space. Hearing footsteps nearing, Tommy quickly joined her.

Bruce arrived just in time to see Tommy's head disappear. "Haley!" he shouted, looking down into the abyss.

"Bruce," Haley's voiced echoed back.

Gripping his gun, he dropped down 8 feet into the unknown. Landing upon damp dirt, a draft hit him. His eyes adjusted to the dimness, as a disturbing image unfolded before him.

Tommy held Haley hostage, placing a gun to her head. His arm was wrapped around her upper belly, hands roving her breasts.

Victor was beside them, holding a gun to another slave's head. Her nude body was rail thin, emaciated. Red sores ringed her wrists, cut from wall-fastened chains. The woman was too weak to fight. She was ragged, dirt-covered. Sandy-soot shielded her dusty face, body, and dark hair.

Bruce slowly approached, gripping his handgun tightly. He only had two bullets, though it was all he needed.

"That's close enough, Mr. Knight," Victor warned.

Bruce spoke loudly, in a threatening manner. "This ends one of two ways. Haley gets released...you live. She dies...you join her. Simple as that."

"Now, Bruce...since when have I been a simple man?" Victor asked with a smirk on his face.

"Make your fucking point."

"I always have options."

"Name them."

"Here's my offer to you. Place your gun down; one of these slaves is spared. Or...you fire that weapon...they both die. Choose."

"Why would I choose a stranger over the woman I love?"

"Because, you love them both. Say hello to *Carolina*."

Bruce gasped in disbelief, as Haley joined him. Victor parted the slave's crusted hair, revealing her tired, lifeless face. As Mr. Cruz blew the dust off her, it revealed a familiar red tone. Her face was swollen, eyes bagged, and spirit drained. However, there was no question. It was her.

Haley cried, knowing Bruce could never choose. Her heart broke for the woman, wondering what life must have been like all those years. Tears rimmed her eyes.

The gun trembled in Bruce's hand. Catching his breath, he asked, "Carolina! Is it really you?"

She fought to speak, straining her voice. "Bruce. I have no life left...let me die."

Victor slapped her. "Shut your damn mouth, slave!"

Anger filled Bruce, as he gripped his gun tighter. "She died *that* night! I held her in my arms...looked in her lifeless eyes!"

Victor nodded. "You're correct. She did die...and I kept my promise of throwing her body to the dogs. However, right before Rico tossed her in, she was revived. The bullet never hit a vital organ...nothing of importance. Seeing your strong-will, I realized what worth she possessed to the right man...at the right moment. I was correct in my assumption."

"The baby? Is it...alive?" Bruce asked.

"As I said...the bullet hit nothing of importance. Though, it did strike the fetus," Victor said with a smirk upon his face.

Fire filled Bruce's eyes, as he screamed, "Mother fucker!"

Tommy's laugh echoed throughout the dungeon, as Victor announced, "Time is running out. Choose now."

"I can't! I won't!"

"Then I'll make your decision easier. At the count of five...they'll both die. Unless, of course, you place your gun down...and give me a name. Comply...and you'll be spared...along with your choice."

"Rotting in some shit hole!" Bruce shouted.

"No. Returned to the island. Maybe returned to my side...in time. After another lesson in loyalty, of course. Enough chatter. One. Two. Three..."

Bruce studied Haley's hurt eyes, as heavy tears streamed downward. *I can't kill her,* he said. *She's got an entire life to live, to love. She's carrying my child.* He thought his decision was made, as he stared into Carolina's lifeless eyes. Although he'd long mourned her, he couldn't bring himself to let her go again.

"Four...five," Victor said. "Your choice is made." He and Tommy prepared to pull the trigger.

"Wait!" Carolina called out.

"A last word before dying?" Victor asked her.

"Free me, Bruce," she said. "Finish what you started." Having once spoken those words on the forest's edge, he understood exactly what she meant. He gazed in her eyes one last time, a wish he'd wanted for years.

Knight aimed the gun at Carolina's chest, firing a bullet directly through it. She gasped, dropping to the sandy floor.

Mr. Cruz expected *her* demise. However, his own end was never considered. A trail of blood spilled from his own chest, in the same spot Carolina was first shot. Blankness filled his eyes, as he toppled over the downed slave.

Haley thrust her elbow into Tommy's stomach. She broke free, ducking. Bruce aimed, firing his last bullet into the scumbag's head.

A hole formed between Tommy's eyes, as he fell backwards from the force. "Bruce!" Haley shouted, running into his safe arms. They both freed Carolina's body from Victor's weight.

Bruce held the dying woman in his arms for the second time. He intentionally missed her vital organs, hoping she'd survive. However, death is more than biological. Her energy faded, as she willed her spirit away.

"Carolina! Please...stay with me!" he begged. "Let me gaze upon you...for one last time."

Her tired eyes reopened, as she said, "I knew you'd come back...someday. I hung on...suffered so much. Though, even through all the torture, starvation, and isolation...I wouldn't have changed a thing. For just the short time we had together, I'd face it all again," she whispered. Turning her weakened head toward Haley, she said, "Take care of him. Give your baby the chance...mine never had."

Ms. White nodded, wiping tears from her eyes.

"Stay with me...just a little longer...please!" Bruce begged.

"There's nothing left for me here. I died that night, along with our love. Goodbye, Bruce...I'm going home," she said, as her energy faded away.

Bruce leaned in, kissing her soiled lips. By the time he withdrew, Carolina was finally free.

*****

Haley and Bruce exited *Paraíso,* never looking back. By the time word got to Venezuelan authorities, the slaves were well in flight. Knight carried Carolina's body into the forest.

Taking the bar's ice shovel, Bruce dug a proper grave. Haley stood close to his side, as he placed an arm around her. The two remained quiet, taking a few moments in silent goodbye. Carolina was the reason they found each other, no matter how hellish the path was.

They moved further into the dark woods. Heading west into Columbia, daybreak painted the sky with hope. Radiant reds and oranges burned the atmosphere, lighting the way forward into freedom. They didn't know what their future held. However, they did know one thing.

As long as Bruce and Haley were together, life would be worth dying for.

Other Books by J.D. Grayson

YOUR FRIENDLY NEIGHBORHOOD BDSM CLUB
Available at: Amazon

After entering the local PTA meeting, Caroline Chase feels out of place. She finds an unwelcoming bunch of ladies, prim and proper in every manner. Owen Hayes, the dapper PTA president, presents the same air of perfection. Too good to be true, she knows the most polished people often hide the dirtiest secrets.

Intrigued by the group's plastic facade, Caroline Chase returns again. It's then, she finds a reality which only existed in her sexual fantasies. Challenged to submit, she'll be forced to face questions of inner strength and willpower. However, Caroline will soon discover, she's not the only one in need of an awakening.

*****

THE PREGNANCY TRANCE
Available at: Amazon

Amber Evans enters a hypnotherapist's office seeking help. Unable to get pregnant, she's desperate to find an answer. Eager to cure her, Bruce Carson examines her subconscious mind, treading a darker path than he expected to walk.

Fighting his own battle of darkness, Bruce hopes redemption lies in Amber's cure. Though to heal her, he'll have to survive the dangerous place it takes him. Obsessed with his mission, he'll even risk his life to deliver the pregnancy trance.

*****

MARRIAGE THERAPY: A DOM, A SUB & A CUCKOLD
Available at: Amazon

Lori and Tyler Hale have a nice home, good jobs, and decent relationship. Though while Tyler is happy to forego bedroom matters, Lori desires a kinky edge. With no answer in sight, the couple turns to marriage therapy.

Recommended by a friend, Dr. Stone welcomes the couple into his office. The Hales soon discover their therapist's unique way of treatment. Using the tools of sexual discipline, he pushes their marriage to the edge. Willing to risk their breaking, he challenges their sexual limits. Though the more he explores his female patient, the more he's tempted to let them fail.

*****

DOCTOR MÉNAGE
Available at: Amazon

Returning to their hometown in style, Doctors Mason & Ross open a sexual medicine practice. Blessed with wealth and good looks, the bachelors are desired by every female in the zip code. Since the girls can't win the doctors' hearts, they must settle for sexual treatment instead.

Attending their high-school reunion, the doctors are approached by a face from their past. The popular and beautiful Kayla Carter seeks them out, hoping they'll cure her sexual dysfunction. Agreeing to treat her, the two doctors make a deal to stimulate her body, but not their hearts. Of course, promises are easier to make than keep.

*****

THE COLONY:
ARRIVAL (PART I)
TEMPTATION (PART II)
PROPHECY (PART III)
ADDICTS (PART IV)
Available at: Amazon, Smashwords, iBooks & B&N

After years of marital heartache, Dylan & Alexa Hunter have lost the will to go on. After being approached by a mysterious man, they are offered a chance to start over in a utopian paradise. The word eternity is spoken, though left undefined.

On the island of Aionios, no fruit is forbidden, no pleasure denied. Accepting the tempting offer, the couple surrenders everything, including freewill itself. Though they'll soon learn that even paradise has a dark side.

*****

THE PATIENT:
PHYSICAL (PART I)
DOUBLE DOSE (PART II)
THE CURE (PART III)
Available at: Amazon, B&N, iBooks, Smashwords, KOBO, Sony, and Diesel

Twenty-two year old, Rebecca Stone is a naive girl with medical anxiety. Having minimal sexual experience, and being submissive in nature, she is prime meat in the hands of horny predators. Sensing her obvious weakness, her new boss demands a pre-employment physical. However, what she doesn't know, is that the doctor's secretly working with him, exploiting timid girls like herself.

Rebecca is forced to face her deep fear of doctors, pulled into a world of medical submission. Along the journey, she will discover the root of her feelings, and gain a newfound fetish in the process.

*****

TEACHING EMMA:
A CONTRACT OF SUBMISSION (PART I)
THE MASTER/SUB EXPERIENCE (PART II)
FREEDOM OF SUBMISSION (PART III)
Available at: Amazon, Smashwords, iBooks & B&N

Emma Heart starts college with an unusual elective: Human Sexuality-Fetish and Lifestyles. She doesn't know that her new teacher, Mark Ryan, is as unusual as the course itself. The class is given a contract of submission, agreeing to become his subs, empowering him their Dom. The lessons that follow will not be learned from books, but bodies.

As he focuses on Emma, Professor Ryan begins to question his own methods. Feeling stronger for his student than expected, he realizes the only outcome is heartbreak. He must decide between love or scholastic duty. The question is...can he?

*****

DOMINATED BY THE BOSS (PART I)
DOMINATED BY THE BOSS (PART II)
Available at: Amazon, B&N, iBooks, Smashwords, KOBO, Sony, and Diesel

After her husband loses his job, Ashley Taylor begins stealing from her company. What starts as petty theft, becomes grand larceny. Caught by her boss, Mrs. Taylor is faced with a simple choice.

Go to federal prison for many years or serve Ethan Cole for one? What appears to be the safe choice becomes a world of domination. Punished for her misdeeds, she'll discover that every dollar must be repaid. However, the currency is not money. It's her sexual freedom.

*****

THE HYPNOTIST: SEX TRANCE
Available at: Amazon

Hoping to cure his wife's bedroom boredom, Sean Day turns to hypnotherapist, Joseph Ryan, to cure his wife. Though, due to Misty's uptight upbringing, the hypnotist is forced to skirt the rules. He lies to her.

Under the guise of smoking addiction treatment, Misty is seduced into trance. Joseph intends to fix her intimacy issues. However, after exploring Misty's dark mind, a deeper issue is revealed. Her words unlock Mr. Ryan's own unspoken fetish, forcing him to break new ground. Pushed to the edge of submission, Mrs. Day will face her shameful secrets, along with the mental bonds that hold her captive.

*****

THE DENTIST: SEDATION
Available at: Amazon

Throughout Dr. Ivy's life, a dark fantasy has tested his limits of self-control. Finally ready to cross the threshold of reality, the allure of exploiting sedated patients claims him. As satisfying as the experience turns out, it fails to cure a lonely heart.

Realizing he requires more than a warm body, the doctor revisits an abandoned idea. Working on numerous formulas, he discovers that the right mix of nitrous oxide will make his dream come true.

Just when his plans are in place, a new regulation forces him to hire a dental assistant. The beautiful Kimberly Carter arrives, watching his every move. It appears his fantasy-driven dreams are thwarted, when he discovers his assistant may share them as well.

*****

THE FANTASY FACTORY:
EDGY ROLE PLAY
Available at: Amazon

Vicky Lane's sex life has hit a wall. Failing to spice things up with sexy outfits and toys, the luscious housewife threatens her husband with an affair. After he carelessly dares her to go forward, Vicky calls Gavin's bluff. Raising the stakes, she lets her dark side shine.

She signs up for the fantasy factory, where fantasy becomes reality. Wanting to act out her darkest taboo, she signs her freedom away, putting it in the hands of unknown men. Taken at random, an edgy adventure follows suit. Vicky hopes to teach Gavin a lesson of her value, though by the end, the lesson will belong to them both.

The Fantasy Factory series will be an occasional series of non-sequential, "Paid for hire" role-play. They can be read in any order.

About J.D. Grayson

All books are now available in Paperback. For autographed copies please send your request to JDGrayson@hotmail.com

Website: www.JDGraysonBooks.com
Twitter: @JDGraysonBooks
Facebook: http://www.facebook.com/JDGraysonBooks

You can contact J.D. Grayson at JDGrayson@hotmail.com

J.D. Grayson lives in the state of Florida, where the heat and sweat naturally lead him to write erotica. Preferring short erotica to long form, he tries to offer a burst of pleasure, while merging an interesting story with a few twists along the journey.

With every work, Grayson attempts to straddle the line of sensuality and kink, story and sex, as well as fantasy and reality. Although sex always leads the way, he strives to add imagination to every plot line, in addition to each sex act. Some stories are lighter in tone, others are darker, though he always aims for a tasteful presentation.

His ultimate goal is to add spice to the life of readers. In his daily conversations with "average couples," he discovered that the current state of sexuality is not in a good place. Somehow, it's been lost in maddening schedules, busy lives, and shamed stereotypes. Its importance and priority are pushed to the back burner, as a chore not a reliever.

If just one of his stories adds some lust to their love, then his mission is accomplished.

www.ingramcontent.com/pod-product-compliance
Lightning Source LLC
Chambersburg PA
CBHW022013170626
46808CB00001B/380